SPUG
THE MAGIC PLANET

Paul Philip Studer

Michael Terence
Publishing

Chapter One

Mitor was soaring in the **thermals** above the snow-capped peaks of the Silothan Mountains. He was gaining height, ready for the long glide down to the Vushy Plains below. When he was satisfied he was high enough, **Mitor** flapped his mighty wings and began the descent.

Mitor was a bird of prey; a big one. His wing span was over ten foot. He had a sharp, hooked beak and vicious looking **talons**. He was a mile high, but his eyesight was so good he could see an ant crawling about on the Plains below. But **Mitor** wasn't hunting ants; he was hunting **The Bonz**.

The Bonz was a rodent, like an overgrown guinea pig. **Mitor** and **The Bonz** had been enemies for centuries. But it was a very respectful war. It was in **Mitor's** interests that **The Bonz** survived and prospered. He always gave them a chance.

Mitor spotted **The Bonz**, folded his wings back and dived. He was travelling at over 200 miles an hour. He should have been smashed to pieces on the Plain below, travelling at such a speed, but this was **Spug**: The Magic Planet. **Mitor** was a magic eagle. He simply flapped his giant wings and landed quietly next to **The Bonz**. The stricken animal froze. **Mitor** spoke to him in a deep voice: 'If **King Aloysius** has a purpose for you, let him magic you away. If not, I will take you back to the Silothan Mountains.'

King Aloysius was **King** of **The Bonz**. He could trace his line back two thousand years to a time when **The Wizards** of **Spug** were dividing the planet into their kingdoms. **The Bonz** came under **Wizard 37**; it was him that gave **The Bonz** their magic.

All the other wizards had names. **Wizard 37** preferred a number; it was less bother. If your name was '**Wizard Gyromuglan**' you had something to live up to, but if your name was plain '**Wizard 37**', people didn't expect much, which suited **Wizard 37** just fine. He liked **The Bonz**. They weren't very bright; they didn't ask questions, and they didn't expect much. In fact, they didn't expect anything at all. **Wizard 37** was happy to give them a bit of magic. He gave them something nobody could argue about: he gave them the magic that enabled them to survive. It had been very successful magic. **The Bonz** were one of the oldest animals on **Spug**.

They had survived for thousands of years, virtually unchanged.

There was a loud 'CRACK'. A large crack appeared in the hard Vushy Plain and **The Bonz** disappeared down it. **The Bonz** landed in a heap, amid a cloud of dust, in the **King's** Chamber. **King Aloysius** was sat on his throne. He wasn't pleased. He said: 'How many times do I have to tell you, **Frodo**, never go out onto the Plain during the day. Dawn and dusk are our times. Dawn and dusk! Goodness knows, I've made you repeat it often enough!'

FRODO: 'But I was bored, **Dad**. It's such a long time between dawn and dusk.'

Boredom wasn't usually a problem with **The Bonz**, as I've said before, they were not that bright. But **Frodo** was **King Aloysius's** son. The **King** was the brightest of his generation. So it was no surprise that his son was a cut above the average **Bonz**.

Queen Fancy came rushing into the **King's** chamber. She said: 'She's gone again, Ally. I put her down for a minute, turned round and there she was, GONE!'

KING ALOYSIUS: 'Calm yourself, **Fancy**, love. Someone will bring her back, they always do. Something more alarming has happened to young **Frodo** here. If **Mitor** had not given me a warning, he would be on his way to the Silothan Mountains by now.'

QUEEN FANCY: 'FRODO! How could you be so careless. We'll never rear them, Ally, we'll never rear them!'

She burst out crying.

KING ALOYSIUS: 'Frodo, go find your sister. She can't have got far.'

He took his wife in his arms and tried to comfort her. **Frodo** was two years old. **The Bonz** generally lived to about 20 years of age, so **Frodo** was the equivalent of an 8 year old in human years. He was at that curious stage, asking questions. Everything was new and exciting; he was always getting into scrapes. His sister, **Mee Bee** was only 6 months old, which put her in the 'terrible twos' in human years. She was into everything. Just lately she had taken to exploring the tunnels that **The Bonz** had burrowed under the Vushy Plain. There were miles of them. These tunnels needed constant maintenance: roots grew into them and the roof

collapsed. **Mee Bee** had driven her **mother,
Queen Fancy**, to **distraction** over the past 4
weeks.

If you had asked any of **The Bonz**, including The
King, to draw a map of their burrows, they couldn't
have done it. But they had this **homing** instinct: no
matter where they were in the burrows, they always
knew which direction was home. Except that this
homing instinct did not fully develop until they
were at least one year old. **Mee Bee** couldn't have
found her way home even if she had wanted to,
which she didn't. She was having too much of a
good time.

Frodo rounded a bend and smelt his sister. He
called out: '**Mee Bee**, is that you?'

MEE BEE: 'Hi **Frodo**, over here. Come and have
a bite of my carrot.'

A wild carrot had grown through into the tunnel. It
wasn't bright orange like the ones we buy, that is
just a Dutch invention. This one was purple and
very sweet. **Mee Bee** moved to one side to let
Frodo in. He took a bite.

FRODO: 'This is good, **Mee Bee**. Have you
found any more of these?'

MEE BEE: 'Yeah, but I couldn't tell you where they are. I can never remember. I just run along until I bump into them.'

FRODO: 'The carrot is good, **Mee Bee**. I can see why you like them. But you shouldn't run off like that. Mum is worried sick.'

MEE BEE: 'What does 'worried' mean?'

FRODO: 'I don't know. It's something adults do. It makes them unhappy. You don't want to make Mum unhappy, do you?'

MEE BEE: 'No, I don't. Do you think I should take her with me and show her the carrot?'

FRODO: 'Yes, that would be a good idea. Come on. Let's go home.'

The first time **Mee Bee** disappeared, **Queen Fancy** had rushed along the burrows, frantically trying to find her. She failed. At tea time one of her Aunties brought **Mee Bee** back, looking dishevelled and slightly **sheepish**. Then it happened again and again. **Queen Fancy** was at her **wits' end**. The last time **Mee Bee** had been gone for two days. **King Aloysius's** sister had brough her back, filthy dirty and looking pleased with herself.

There is a good reason why **Frodo** and **Mee Bee** were brighter than the average **Bonz** children. **Wizard 37** realised that **The Bonz** would not survive by relying on his magic alone; someone needed to have a **modicum** of sense to keep the show on the road. So he set up what he called: '**The Bonz Conundrums**': a device that ensured that only the brightest of **The Bonz** became **King** and ruled the colony.

The Bonz Conundrums could not be run underground. It had to be staged on the Vushy Plain, during the day, in full view of **The Bonz's** many predators, which would have been suicidal. **Wizard 37** came up with a typical **Spug** solution to the problem: he negotiated a deal with **Wizard Gyromuglan**.

Wizard Gyromuglan agreed that all the **Mitors** in the Silothan Mountains would turn from hunters to protectors and guarantee the safety of **The Bonz** whilst they competed in **The Bonz Conundrums**.

THE BONZ

CONUNDRUMS

Chapter Two

There were three **Bonz Conundrums** altogether. They were conducted inside a 320 foot diameter stone circle. There were 75 standing stones and perched on top of every other stone was a **Mitor**. Every other **Mitor** faced inwards, protecting **The Bonz** competing in the **Bonz Conundrum**; and every other **Mitor** faced outwards, protecting **The Bonz** supporters.

The Conundrums were not time trials as such, but they had to be completed in the day. If you didn't complete them all, you were disqualified. **The Bonz** territory on the Vushy Plain was divided into four quarters and each quarter was divided into two halves. Each half nominated one male and one female champion: 16 in total. These 16 champions would compete in **The Bonz Conundrums**.

Each champion was given a sealed wooden box with his/her name on it. A small hole was cut in the top of the box. Scoring used small, coloured stones and small, coloured wooden counters.

Each **Conundrum** had a colour:

CONUNDRUM ONE: RED

CONUNDRUM TWO: AMBER

CONUNDRUM THREE: GREEN

Each box was placed at the foot of a standing stone and guarded by a **Mitor**.

CONUNDRUM ONE: PT : RED

6 trials were set up inside the stone circle. There was no set sequence to complete the trials, so long as you did them all. If you missed one out, or did one twice, as happened sometimes, you were disqualified.

TRIAL ONE: *3 inch jump*
TRIAL TWO: *6 inch jump*
TRIAL THREE: *12 inch jump*

If you cleared a jump, you got a red stone. If you knocked the jump down, you got a red wood.

TRIAL FOUR: *6 foot high climbing net*

If you managed to climb up the net and down the other side, you got a red stone. If you managed to climb one side, then fell off, you got a red wood.

If you froze and had to be rescued, you were disqualified. **The Bonz** were only a foot long, so the 6 foot high climbing net was 36 foot high in human measure; a frightening height.

TRIAL FIVE: The Burrows

Inside a mound of earth were six burrows, but you could only get through three of them. The other three were blocked off with wooden bungs. You couldn't work out which burrows were blocked by watching the other champions as the **Umpire** switched the bungs around for each champion. The burrows were numbered 1 to 6.

If you ran through a burrow and out the other end, you got a red stone. If your way was blocked by a bung, you got a red wood. Some champions were so wound up they ran full pelt into a burrow, crashed into the bung and knocked themselves out. When, after a few minutes, he hadn't come out, one of his supporters went in and rescued him. He was disqualified, of course; couldn't be anything else. He was out cold.

*TRIAL SIX: **Zip Wire***

A log was angled up at 45 degrees, 8 foot high. At the top of the log was a **zip wire** that led down to a post 2 foot high. Attached to the **zip wire** was a pair of handlebars. You had to grab hold of the handlebars, jump off the log, ride down the **zip wire** until you were over the target, then let go. If you scored a 'bull's eye' and landed in the middle of the target, on the red circle, you got a red stone. If you landed within the white outer circle, you got a red wood. If you missed the target altogether, you were disqualified. You had three attempts; you chose your best one.

CONUNDRUM TWO:
BOLT : AMBER

A crossbow was set up which fired a bolt. Arranged across the stone circle were five targets. Each target consisted of an apple mounted in front of a 6 inch square back plate.

- The first target was one foot away, on the ground.

- The second target was two foot away, one foot high.

- The third target was four foot away, two foot high.

- The fourth target was eight foot away, four foot high.

- The fifth target was sixteen foot away, eight foot high.

- If you hit the apple you got an amber stone.

- If you hit the back plate, you got an amber wood.

- If you missed the target completely, you were disqualified. You had three attempts; you chose your best one.

CONUNDRUM THREE:
QUESTIONS : GREEN

QUESTION 1
How many standing stones are there in the circle?

QUESTION 2
How many champions were disqualified in **Conundrum** One?

QUESTION 3
Which number burrow did you go down in **Conundrum** One, Trial 5?

QUESTION 4
How many champions were disqualified in
Conundrum Two?

QUESTION 5
In **Conundrum** Two, how high was the fourth
target?

These simple questions would be quite easy for us,
but **The Bonz** were not known for their brain
power. There was psychology here: the champions
that had made it this far had got through all the
physical trials; all they had to do was answer a few
simplequestions. They relaxed and congratulated
themselves; they had made it, or so they thought.
The questions may be simple, but they were sudden
death: get one wrong and you were out,
disqualified. You had fallen at the final hurdle. It's
surprising how many of the champions who had
done really well in the trials slipped up and gave a
wrong answer because they weren't concentrating.
Quite often it was this so called 'easy' **Conundrum**
Three that decided who would be the next **King**
and **Queen** of **The Bonz**. A true champion does
not lose concentration and slow down as he
approaches the finishing line. He keeps going right
to the end and makes sure of victory.

No green wood was handed out in **Conundrum** Three. If you answered all the questions correctly, you got one green stone. It was the most valued stone in the competition. You couldn't become **King** or **Queen** of **The Bonz** without it.

When everyone had finished, the boxes of the champions who had completed all three **Conundrums** were opened and the stones and woods counted. Whoever had the most stones and the least woods was declared the overall champion: one male, one female. There was a short courting period – usually about a month. If they liked each other, they married and became **King** and **Queen** of **The Bonz**. If they really could not get on, they would choose the champion who had finished in second place. The two couples were then asked a **Conundrum** Three question. Again, it was sudden death. If they got it wrong, they were disqualified. The questions continued until one couple gave a wrong answer.

Three was no male preference: if the male **Bonz** and his second placed mate won, they would become **King** and **Queen**. If the female **Bonz** and her second placed mate won, the female **Bonz** would become **Queen** and rule the colony and her mate would be given the title of **The Duke of Vushy**.

If a brother and sister both won, they were not allowed to marry each other; that would be **incest. Incest** was banned on **Spug**. Instead they were each paired up with the second placed champion. After a short courting period - usually about a month – if they liked each other, each couple were asked a **Conundrum** Three question. Again, it was sudden death. If they gave a wrong answer, they were disqualified and the other couple went on to be **King** and **Queen** or **Queen** and **The Duke of Vushy**. If one couple could not get on, the other couple went on to become **King** and **Queen** or **Queen** and **The Duke of Vushy**, without having to answer any more simple questions.

That's how **Wizard 37** ensured that only the most able **Bonz** ruled the colony.

Wizard 37 was the oldest of the wizards on **Spug**. He beat **Wizard Gyromuglan** by seven days. Generally, wizards lived to about a thousand years old, but **Wizard 37** was twice that. The secret of his long life was simple: he did **nowt**. He just became old and **crabby.**

Chapter Three

The old **King Cyrus** had died. His wife, **Queen Bee**, had called on **Wizard 37** with the bad news.

WIZARD 37: 'I'm sorry, **Bee**. He was a good **King**. One of the best we've had, I'd say. You know what this means?'

QUEEN BEE: 'Yes. **The Bonz Conundrums** will have to be staged again. Why does it have to be so quick?'

WIZARD 37: '**The Bonz** need a leader. They are a bit like sheep; they can't think for themselves. Most of them can't anyway; they need someone to follow. Time is of the **essence**. Don't worry, we'll give **Cyrus** a good send-off.'

———————

All four Quarters were busy frantically trying to decide who will be their champions. They hadn't got the protection of the **Mitors** yet, so they couldn't hold their own **Conundrums** on the Vushy Plains. They would be fair game for any of their predators if they did that. **The Bonz** had a lot of predators. So they were out at dawn and dusk, their usual times on the Vushy Plain, running races, jumps, throwing stones. A group of the older **Bonz** had put their heads together to try and come up with some questions to ask the candidates, but they kept falling asleep.

Wizard 37 visited all four Quarters and gathered the names of all sixteen champions who would compete in **The Bonz Conundrums**. The list was as follows.

FIRST QUARTER CHAMPIONS:

First Half: Male: Aloysius

     Female: Biddy

Second Half: Male: Reeve

     Female: Quallow

SECOND QUARTER CHAMPIONS:

First Half: Male: Pike

     Female: Livey

Second Half: Male: Pluto

     Female: Venus

THIRD QUARTER CHAMPIONS:

First Half: Male: Numpty

     Female: Indy

Second Half: Male: Trev

     Female: Fancy

FOURTH QUARTER CHAMPIONS:
First Half: Male: Plato
               Female: Ping
Second Half: Male: Crust
               Female: Nooloo

The **Bonz Conundrums** started at dawn. **Aloysius** and the other champions were stood just inside the stone circle, waiting for the **Umpire** to fire the starting gun. The **Umpire** was **Professor Rumpant Pustule**, an **anthropologist** from Fartigen University. He had studied **The Bonz** for 30 years. This was his second **Bonz Conundrums**; he had witnessed the **Conundrums** when **Cyrus** and **Bee** had won. **Professor Rumpant Pustule** was 59. This would probably be his last **Bonz Conundrums**. He was looking forward to it.

Anthropologists normally study human beings, but **Rumpant** had stumbled upon **The Bonz** during his gap year, when he was travelling around **Spug**. He was incredibly lucky with his timing: **The Bonz Conundrums** were due to be staged in 3 days' time. He was amazed at what these brown, furry animals got up to. The behaviour was very human- like. They could even speak English. You could have a conversation with a **Bonz**. It was easy to forget that you were talking to a brown furry animal. Actually, they weren't all brown; they varied from black to ginger.

Wizard 37 umpired that first **Bonz Conundrum** that **Rumpant** saw, but it was getting a bit too much for him. **Rumpant** decided to study **The Bonz** at university. He wrote his thesis on them for his PhD. Every summer, he was in the Vushy Plain with his notebook, scribbling away. When **The Bonz Conundrums** were to be held again, **Wizard 37** asked **Rumpant** to **Umpire** them. He leapt at the chance.

Aloysius would be the first one off. As the old **King Cyrus's** son, he was one of the favourites. His parents had both won **The Bonz Conundrums**. They were the brightest of their generation, but it didn't always follow. **Cyrus** and **Bee** had both been outsiders:

Cyrus came from the first half of the fourth Quarter and **Bee** came from the second half of the first Quarter.

Aloysius kept looking up nervously at the **Mitor's** perched on top of the standing stones. There were more of them than he knew existed. All his life, he had been taught to fear the **Mitor**. Now, here he was surrounded by them. As usual his **mother, Queen Bee** knew what he was thinking. She could read him like a book. She said: 'Don't worry, **Ally**. **Wizard 37** has done a deal with **Wizard Gyromuglan**. If any of the **Mitors** so much as touch a **Bonz**, they will lose their magic.'

Such a thing was unthinkable on **Spug**: The Magic Planet.

Aloysius was thinking about what his **mother** had said when the **Umpire** fired the starting gun. He jumped and ran the wrong way out of the stone circle. His sister stopped him and pointed him back the right way. As he passed his **mother**, she said: 'Not a good start, **Ally**.'

Aloysius cleared the first jump and crashed into the second. His **mother** came running over to him.

QUEEN BEE: 'Calm down, **Ally**. You can do this. Just take it steady; one trial at a time. Remember the hare and the tortoise. It was the tortoise that won the race. You don't have to be quick, just be accurate. Now take a good run up and clear this third jump. Don't think about the climbing net. Just crawl up it – one pace at a time – and you'll be alright.'

Aloysius followed his **mother's** advice and started to do better. Spectators were not allowed to coach the champions but no one was going to argue with **Queen Bee**. I mean, she was the **Queen**.

Biddy went next. She cleared the first three jumps, but made the mistake of looking down when she was half way up the climbing net on Trial 4. She froze. Her family and friends shouted encouragement, but it was no use. She wouldn't budge. The **Umpire** told her father to go and fetch her down, which he did. **Biddy's Conundrum** had ended before it had hardly begun. She wasn't sorry. She didn't want to do it in the first place. It was her **mother's** idea. She had **delusions of grandeur**.

Reeve and **Quallow** were brother and sister. They had overheard what **Queen Bee** said to **Aloysius** and were taking it slow and steady. It was good advice. They both reached Trial 6 without mishap.

Pike charged around the trials like a mad thing. He ran head-long into Burrow 3, crashed into the wooden bung and knocked himself out. After a while, when it became obvious he wasn't coming out, the **Umpire** told Baz, **Pike's** younger brother, to go and see what had happened to him Baz dragged **Pike** out of the burrow and laid him on the grass in front of one of the standing stones. He was out cold. His father looked down on him and said: 'Stupid boy!'

Indy also came up against a bung in burrow 1, but she managed to stop herself in time. She backed out and collected a red wood; her second of the competition. She had knocked over the very first 3 inch jump in trial 1 and was trying hard not to get carried away like **Pike** had done. But she was terrified of the **zip wire** in trial 6. She held onto the handlebars for dear life and wouldn't let go. **Consequently**, she missed the target completely, hit the two foot post at the bottom and knocked herself out. The St John Ambulance people came rushing over, put her on a stretcher and carried her off to the Doctors' Tent. She really had hit that post with quite a **wallop**.

The remaining champions refused, point blank, to go on the **zip wire**. **The Bonz** may not be over bright, but they were not stupid, apart from **Pike**. The **Umpire** and **Wizard 37** had a **conflab**. A mattress was fetched and tied to the two foot high post at the bottom. Still, the champions refused to take part. So, amazingly, **Wizard 37** calmly walked up to the top of the log, grabbed hold of the handlebars and rode down the **zip wire.**

He deliberately held onto the handlebars until he collided with the post, as **Indy** had done, except the post was now cushioned by a mattress. **Wizard 37** calmly picked himself up, dusted himself down and said: 'Nothing to it.'

The champions were ashamed that this frail old man had shown them up. They had no alternative but to take part in Trial 6: The **zip wire**. But before they did, the **Umpire g**ave them some good advice. He told them exactly where to let go of the handlebars so that they hit the target. He shouldn't have done it really. It gave them an advantage over the champions who had gone before them. So, to even things up, he allowed the others to re-take the **zip wire**, if they wanted to. Without that, **The Bonz Conundrums** would have ended in shambles.

Following the **Umpire's** instructions, most of the champions managed to hit the target at least once, apart from **Numpty** who was so frightened of hitting the post, he kept letting go of the handlebars too early. He did it twice and refused his third go. He was disqualified, much to his relief.

You probably think **Wizard 37** was a brave old stick for riding down the **zip wire** like that. He wasn't really. Wizards have a force field that protects them. He didn't feel a thing.

Aloysius was having trouble with the crossbow in **Conundrum** two : Bolt. He had discovered that it had a **hair trigger**. His first two bolts had thudded into the grass in front of Target one, before he was ready. In no time at all, he found himself in trouble again. If he missed this third go, that would be it. He would be out, disqualified. Very **gingerly,** he moved the crossbow with the tips of his paws, keeping well away from the trigger. He squinted down the length of the crossbow and carefully lined up the tip of the bolt with the centre of the apple. When he could do no more, he held his breath and touched the trigger: 'THWAPP', the bolt shot straight through the centre of the apple. His supporters cheered and **Aloysius** breathed a sigh of relief. 'This is ridiculous,' he thought. 'I'm a nervous wreck and I've only completed the first target. There are four more to go! I'll never make it at this rate.' He tried to calm himself down and think about what his **mother** had said. He looked around but she was nowhere to be seen.

Aloysius soldiered on, taking exaggerated care lining up the second target. 'THWAPP'. Straight through the apple. 'THWAPP'. Straight through the apple on the third target. He started to relax and grinned at his supporters, giving them the thumbs up. 'I don't know what I was worried about,' he thought. 'This is easy.' Fatal mistake. He missed the fourth target. He didn't understand it. He was sure he had lined up the crossbow correctly, yet the bolt had passed underneath the target. He tried again, taking exaggerated care, as before, carefully lining up the tip of the bolt with the centre of the apple. He took a couple of steps back and tried to calm himself. He checked the **sight** for a third time and touched the trigger. The bolt sailednderneath the target, almost an inch below; worse than his first go.

Aloysius didn't know what to do. As with the first target, if he missed his third go, he would be disqualified. He decided to ask the **Umpire** for some time out. He was allowed to do that under the rules. He walked away from the crossbow, around the stone circle, till he was stood sideways on to the **Conundrum** Two : Bolt.

Pluto stepped up to take his place in **Conundrum** Two : Bolt. He was a big, strong lad, full of confidence. He had sailed round the **Conundrums** so far. He handled the crossbow as if he had been doing it all his life. With the minimum of fuss, he shot the bolt right through the centre of the apple on the first three targets, no problem. **Aloysius** was impressed. He had a clear view of the bolt. It went straight and true. **Pluto** was making him look like a fool.

Pluto put another bolt in the crossbow and aimed at the fourth target. He struck the trigger firmly and the bolt sailed underneath the target, just as **Aloysius's** had done. **Pluto** was not best pleased. He **glowered** at the **Umpire**, put another bolt in the crossbow and tried again. Same result. **Pluto** was losing his temper now. He shouted at the **Umpire**: 'Enjoying yourself are yer? Pity it's not your head I'm aiming at. I couldn't miss that!'

He slammed another bolt in the crossbow, took aim and fired. The bolt passed a good two inches underneath the target. **Pluto** shouted: 'It's a fix! I demand a re-trial **Umpire**. You've rigged this crossbow. You must have done. There's no way I could miss by so much!'

Professor Rumpant Pustule, the **Umpire**, was not surprised at this outburst. In fact, he had been expecting it. He had had run-ins with **Pluto's** family before. They had tried to get rid of him on more than one occasion. During his first summer in the Vushy Plains, **Rumpant** was observing a group of young **Bonz** play fighting. He was busy writing in his notebook, describing the scene. When he looked up, he was surprised to find himself surrounded by an angry looking group of adult **Bonz**. They shouted: 'Clear off, you are not wanted here! Go back where you came from.' They were stood on their hind legs, waving their paws at him. Now, **The Bonz** are only about a foot tall when they are stood on their hind legs. That's an average height. **Pluto's** family were slightly bigger than that. In fact, they were the biggest **Bonz** on the Vushy Plain. And they were strong. **The Bonz** needed to be strong to dig their burrows, but **Pluto's** family were especially strong. **Rumpant** looked around him and thought: 'If they knock me to the ground, I am in trouble.' So he said: 'Hey, cool it guys. It's no problem. I'll get out of your hair, no offence, you know. I'm just a student. I just find you interesting, you know. If you don't like it, fine. I'm outta here.'

Pluto's family had never heard this kind of talk before. They didn't understand what. **Rumpant** was saying, so they gave him the benefit of the doubt and let him go.

Rumpant thought that was it. His study of **The Bonz** was over before it had hardly begun; until he bumped into **Wizard 37** and described his encounter with **Pluto's** family. **Wizard 37** took him into his house and told him to sit down. He disappeared into a cupboard. There was the sound of a lot of rooting about and muttering.

Eventually, **Wizard 37** emerged carrying a knobbly old walking stick. He handed it to **Rumpant**.

WIZARD 37: 'If you have any more trouble with **Pluto's** family, point the stick at them and press that knobble there. That should sort them out. Don't let them put you off studying **The Bonz**. It's none of their business. We want you here. In fact, we are flattered that you are taking an interest in us.'

Wizard 37 had spoken as if he was a **Bonz**, which, I suppose, he was in a way. An **honorary Bonz**. **Rumpant** continued with is study of **The Bonz** but he kept well out of the way of **Pluto's** family territory. But they **sought** him out anyway. He was observing a group of **Bonz** in the Third Quarter when they surrounded him again. **Rumpant** pointed the walking stick that **Wizard 37** had given him, at one of **The Bonz** and pressed the knobble. A spark shot out of the end, hit **The Bonz** and knocked him flat on his back, writhing in agony. **Pluto's** family were shocked. They had never seen anything like it before. They were used to getting their own way. But, like all bullies when you stand up to them, they backed away. From then on, they continued to hassle **Rumpant**, but they did it from a safe distance.

Chapter Four

PLUTO: 'It's a fix! I demand a re-trial. You've rigged this crossbow, **Umpire**. You must have done. There's no way I could miss by so much!'

Professor Rumpant Pustule came ambling up. He was carrying his knobbly walking stick. He said: 'It's no fix, son. You blew it. Git outta here. You want me to zap you?' **Pluto** eyed up the knobbly walking stick. He had never been zapped with it himself, but his Dad had told him about it. He didn't like the sound of it.

PLUTO: 'I'll get you for this, **Pustule**. That's a threat, not a promise.' The **Professor** raised his walking stick and pointed it at **Pluto**. He ran.

Aloysius had been calmly watching all this from the side. He had observed the flight of **Pluto's** bolts: they went straight and true to the first three targets, but on the fourth target, the bolt dipped in its flight about two foot from the target. That's why it missed. **Aloysius** tried to think what this meant. He was not a natural thinker, but his father, **King Cyrus**, had trained him in the art of thinking. He could do it, but he had to concentrate very hard. He thought: 'The target is 6 inches square, the bolt passed underneath the target by about an inch. That meant that the bolt had dipped by $3 + 1 = 4$ inches. So, if he aimed the bolt an inch above the target, he should hit the apple.

Aloysius walked up to the crossbow and indicated to the **Umpire** that he was ready to carry on. He carefully lined the bolt up with the centre of the apple on Target 4, then squinted along the centre of the crossbow and pointed the tip of the bolt at an imaginary point an inch above the target. It felt weird. It didn't feel right at all. His instinct was to point the bolt at the apple, but he held his nerve and touched the trigger. 'THWAPP' – straight through the centre of the apple. His supporters cheered and **Aloysius** breathed a sigh of relief.

One more target to go. He had a plan for that. He carefully lined up the crossbow on Target 5 and pointed the bolt at the apple. He focused his eyes on the target and at the same time, touched the trigger. He watched very carefully as the bolt sailed underneath the target. **Aloysius** reckoned it had passed about a foot below. Using the same principle as before, that meant to hit the apple, he would have to aim a foot above the target. He wasn't so worried this time. It was only his second go. He had one more left. He squeezed the trigger and the bolt just nicked the top of the apple. He was safe. He was assured of at least an amber wood, but he thought he could go one better. He concentrated: the apple was about 2 inches in diameter. So, if he wanted to hit the centre of it, he had to lower the bolt by an inch. He took aim again and tried to judge a point eleven inches above the target. He took his time. When he was ready, he touched the trigger: 'THWAPP'; straight through the centre of the apple.

His supporters cheered. **Aloysius** waved to them and allowed himself a little smile. He had made it through to **Conundrum** Three : Questions. He was within touching distance of the prize. But now, he had his 'thinking cap' on, he had to keep it there. **King Cyrus** couldn't coach his son on the questions – they changed with each set of **Conundrums**; but he told him he must concentrate hard and listen very carefully. The questions were **deceptively** easy and very easy to get wrong. He told him not to say the first thing that came into his head. Take his time; make sure his answer was right before giving it. It was easier to fail on **Conundrum** Three than all the other trials put together.

———————

Seven **Bonz** had made it through to **Conundrum** Three. They were:

> MALE: **Aloysius, Reeve, Crust**
> FEMALE: **Quallow, Venus, Fancy, Ping**

Wizard 37 and **Wizard Gyromuglan** helped **Umpire Professor Rumpant Pustule** ask the questions. The **Professor** took **Aloysius, Reeve** and **Quallow. Wizard 37** took **Venus** and **Fancy** and **Wizard Gyromuglan** took **Crust** and **Ping**.

Each contestant was asked the questions individually. There was no **conferring. Aloysius** went first.

UMPIRE: 'How many stones are there in the stone circle?'

Aloysius thought it was a trick question. The stones were right there in front of him. All he had to do was count them. Maybe that's what his father meant when he said they were **deceptively** easy.

He counted the stones, then made himself count them again before he gave his answer: '75'.

UMPIRE: 'Correct. How many champions were disqualified in **Conundrum** One?' **Aloysius** thought back to **Conundrum** One. There was **Biddy, Pike, Indy, Numpty**. He was going to give the answer '4', but something stopped him. What had happened to **Nooloo**? She definitely didn't compete in **Conundrum** Two, but he hadn't seen her disqualified in **Conundrum** One either; she had just disappeared. He went over it all again in his head. He was positive that **Nooloo** hadn't competed in **Conundrum** Two. He had watched all the other champions on the crossbow and she never fired a bolt. So she must have been disqualified in **Conundrum** One.

Aloysius knew the importance of his answer; if he got it wrong, he could forget about following in his father's footsteps and becoming **King**. He closed his eyes, took a deep breath, and said, quietly: '5'.

The **Umpire's** voice rang out loud and clear: 'Correct!'

UMPIRE: 'Which number burrow did you go down in **Conundrum** One, trial 5?' **Aloysius** knew the answer straight away, but he remembered his father's advice: 'Don't say the first thing that comes into your head.' So he bit his lip and thought … Yes, he was sure he was right.

ALOYSIUS: 'Burrow 2'

UMPIRE: 'Correct! How many champions were disqualified in **Conundrum** Two?'

Aloysius thought back to **Conundrum** Two: there was **Pluto**, of course, **Livey**, **Trev** and **Plato**. All the others had got through, he was sure of it. Nevertheless, he went over it all again before he gave his answer: '4'.

UMPIRE: 'Correct. In **Conundrum** Two, how high was the fourth target?' **Aloysius** had had plenty of time to study the targets in **Conundrum** Two when he was watching **Pluto** shoot his bolts. He knew the answer and blurted out: 'Four foot', in his excitement, forgetting all his previous caution. Fortunately the **Umpire** said: 'Correct'.

Aloysius had made it. He had completed all three **Conundrums**. There was nothing more he could do. It all depended now on how many woods and stones he had.

———————————

I should explain about **Nooloo**. She had been disqualified on a technicality. She had gone with her best friend, **Indy**, to the Doctor's Tent when she hit the post at the bottom of the **zip wire**. She stayed with her for the rest of the afternoon, holding her paw. She took no further part in the **Conundrums**, even though she had done very well with 100% success, collecting 5 red stones for the trials she had completed. She could well have won if she had carried on.

Question 2 on **Conundrum** Three was catching most of the champions out. They gave the answer: '4', which, on the ground was right. But they didn't know about **Nooloo**. So far, only **Aloysius** had managed to work it out.

The other 6 **Bonz** champions had all been fitted with headphones, so that they couldn't hear each other's answers and the **Umpire**, **Wizard 37** and **Wizard Gyromuglan** had spaced themselves a good distance apart, so there was no chance of cheating, not by the champions anyway.

Wizard 37 pointed at **Venus**. She came forward to take her turn. No one from **Number 22** had made it this far before. They were all excited, especially **Pluto**. **Wizard 37** removed **Venus's** headphones and asked her the first Question: 'How many standing stones are there in the stone circle?'

Venus looked around, counted the stones, and answered confidently: '75'.

WIZARD 37: 'Correct. How many champions were disqualified in **Conundrum** One?'

Venus thought for a few minutes and answered confidently: '4'.

WIZARD 37: 'Wrong.'

Venus screamed at the top of her voice: 'NO!'

She launched herself at **Wizard 37**, knocking him to the ground.

The St John's Ambulance people came running over, lifted her off **Wizard 37** and carried her, still kicking and screaming, to the Doctor's Tent, where she was given a sedative.

Fancy came running over and helped **Wizard 37** to his feet. She was the next one to be questioned. She said: 'Are you alright, sir? Do you want some time out to recover? Can I get you a drink or something?'

WIZARD 37: 'Thank you for your concern, my dear. I'm alright. No harm done. We don't look it, but us **wizards** are a pretty tough bunch, you know.'

FANCY: 'She's a wild one is that **Venus**. Imagine if we had her for Queen! She'd be falling out with everyone!'

WIZARD 37: 'Quite! It doesn't bear thinking about. Are you ready for your Questions, **Fancy**?'

FANCY: 'Yes – well, as ready as I'll ever be. I don't hold out much hope.'

WIZARD 37: 'Don't put yourself down so much, my dear. You are a good lady. You know what they always say: 'Good will out!' Right, Question One: How many standing stones are there in the stone circle?'

Like **Aloysius**, **Fancy** thought it was a trick question. The stones were right there in front of her. All she had to do was count them. She shrugged, counted the stones, and gave the answer: '75'.

WIZARD 37: 'Correct. How many champions were disqualified in **Conundrum** One?' **Fancy** thought back to **Conundrum** One. There was **Pike**, **Biddy**, **Numpty**, and of course poor **Indy**. She was worried about **Indy**. She was about to answer '4' when **Wizard 37** looked her in the eye and shook his head very slightly. He put his right hand up to the side of his head and spread out his five fingers.

Fancy was a bright girl, she had to be to get this far. She realised that **Wizard 37** was trying to tell her something. But she didn't see how the answer could be five. She was positive only four had been disqualified. Nevertheless, she trusted **Wizard 37** and gave the answer: '5'.

WIZARD 37: 'Correct!'

With **Wizard 37's** help, **Fancy** managed to answer all the rest of the questions correctly. Was **Wizard 37** right to help **Fancy**? Who would you prefer as Queen: **Venus** or **Fancy**? I know who I would fancy: **Fancy**!

———————————

Only four of the champions completed all three **Conundrums**: **Reeve** and **Quallow**, **Aloysius** and **Fancy**.

They opened **Reeve's** box first. It contained:

REEVE: 6 red stones, 3 amber stones, 2 amber woods, 1 green stone

QUALLOW: 6 red stones, 3 amber stones, 2 amber woods, 1 green stone

FANCY: 5 red stones, 1 red wood, 4 amber stones, 1 amber wood, 1 green stone

ALOYSIUS: 5 red stones, 1 red wood, 5 amber stones, 1 green stone. The scoring is as follows:

Red wood:	1 point
Red stone:	2 points
Amber wood:	2 points
Amber stone:	4 points
Green stone:	8 points

Which gave:

REEVE:	36 points
QUALLOW:	36 points
FANCY:	37 points
ALOYSIUS:	39 points

which made **Aloysius King elect** and **Fancy** Queen **elect**.

Their supporters mobbed them, held them **aloft** and paraded them around the stone circle.

Chapter Five

Wizard 37 and **Professor Rumpant Pustule** were sat in the sun, in pink and white striped deckchairs, in **Wizard 37's** back garden, supping mugs of tea and dunking custard creams.

RUMPANT: 'All's well that ends well, eh 37?'

WIZARD 37: 'Aye, you could say that. It were a close-run thing though.'

RUMPANT: 'You mean **Venus**?'

WIZARD 37: 'Absolutely! You could have knocked me down with a feather when I saw her stood standing there. No one from **Number 22** has ever made it to **Conundrum** Three before. Bye, I was pleased when she got that question wrong.'

Rumpant laughed and said: 'I thought she was going to kill ya!'

WIZARD 37: 'It's not so easy to kill a wizard.'

RUMPANT: 'Why don't you just ban **Number 22** from the **Conundrums**?'

WIZARD 37: 'I can't do that. It has to be open access for it to work. We need **Number 22** in the

gene pool to keep **The Bonz** physically strong. But it's a worry. They have always been a handful. Imagine if **Venus** had become Queen!'

RUMPANT: 'I pity **Aloysius**. She would have made his life hell!'

WIZARD 37: 'Aye, there is that. But what worries me is their ambition. **Number 22** have never been satisfied with their territory. They are always trying to expand it, picking fights with their neighbours. I've had to bring them back into line several times over the years. If one of them gets to be King or Queen, they could declare war on **The Highland Bonz**.'

RUMPANT: 'I've heard talk of **The Highland Bonz**, but I've never seen one.'

WIZARD 37: 'No, you won't. They are **nocturnal**. They will only see me if I make an appointment in writing and give them plenty of notice.'

RUMPANT: 'Are they the same as the Vushy Plain **Bonz**?'

WIZARD 37: 'No, they are smaller. About half the size, and they have a little tuft on their heads.

They wouldn't stand a chance against the Vushy Plain **Bonz**.'

RUMPANT: 'Sounds bad, man. Can't you just change **The Bonz Conundrums**? Make it more difficult for **Number 22** – they are **not the sharpest knife in the drawer**.'

WIZARD 37: 'The only one I'm allowed to change is **Conundrum** Three : Questions. Those are different every time. But if I make the questions harder, there is a danger that none of **The Bonz** will get them right.'

RUMPANT: 'Why can't you alter **Conundrums** One and Two?'

WIZARD 37: 'They have to have the official **sanction** of **The Grand Council of Wizards**. If I want to change them, we will have to **reconvene** the **Grand Council**. What a **palaver** that is! The last time we did it was 20 years ago when **Wizard Gyromuglan** had a problem with a **rogue Mitor** who was killing **Bonz willy nilly**. **Wizard Gyromuglan** wanted to have the **Mitor** destroyed but **The Grand Council of Wizards** wouldn't let him. Instead they transferred the **Mitor** to Upper ppa pupa people, uppappa pata puple, upper pata popacutle …

RUMPANT: 'Are you trying to say Upper Poppleton Castle?'

WIZARD 37: 'Absolutely. I can never say that name. Any road up, the **Mitor** did very well at … that castle what you have just said, entertaining the tourists. **Wizard Gyromuglan** has been supplying them with **Mitors** ever since.

RUMPANT: 'All's well that ends well.' **WIZARD 37**: 'You've said that before.' **RUMPANT**: 'Absolutely.'

WIZARD 37: 'Has 'Yes' been replaced by 'Absolutely'?'

RUMPANT: 'Absolutely!' They both laughed at that.

WIZARD 37: 'Seriously, though, **The Bonz Conundrums** have done pretty well what I designed them to do over the years. They have provided us with some very good Kings and Queens of **The Bonz**. Apart from **Arbuthnot** – he was hopeless!'

RUMPANT: 'What was the matter with **Arbuthnot**?'

WIZARD 37: 'He could never make up his mind. Worse, when he did eventually make up his mind, he changed it again. No one knew what to do. It was chaos.'

RUMPANT: 'When was this?'

WIZARD 37: 'About a thousand years ago.'
RUMPANT: 'Ah, quite recent then?'

WIZARD 37: '**Indubitably.**'

RUMPANT: 'There is an old saying: 'If it ain't broke, don't fix it'!'

WIZARD 37: 'I agree with that. **The Bonz Conundrums** are not broke. They provide a good examination of physical fitness, courage, skill, and an ability to think. They do not need fixing. But if one of **Number 22's** family did win, I would ask for **The Grand Council of Wizards** to be **reconvened**. It may be a bit of a **cumbersome** organisation, but there is over a hundred thousand years of experience in that Council. Between them, they have seen most things. They have an **unerring knack** of being able to come up with the right solution to a problem - once you have stopped them talking. The trouble is we don't see each other very often. **The Grand Council of**

Wizards is a perfect opportunity for a good old **chin wag**. I'd say 80% of The Grand Council is taken up with chat and 20% with business, but it works. I've never known them to fail.'

RUMPANT: 'How is **Indy**, by the way? I keep meaning to ask.'

WIZARD 37: 'She's ok, no bones broken. **The Bonz** are surprisingly tough little animals. She's back home now. You'll never guess who's looking after her?'

RUMPANT: 'I thought **Nooloo** was looking after her.'

WIZARD 37: 'She was, but **Queen Bee's** sitting with her now. She seems to have taken to **Indy**. It wouldn't surprise me if she moved in with her. Now that **Aloysius** and **Fancy** are due to be crowned King and Queen, she has **nowt** to do. She's gone from being a **VIB** to **surplus to requirements**, overnight. Plus I think she feels a bit like a **gooseberry**, with **Aloysius** and **Fancy** all over each other.'

Professor Rumpant Pustule was packing up his faithful donkey, **QED**, ready for the long trek back over the Silothan mountains to Fartigen University.

WIZARD 37: 'You coming back for the coronation?'

RUMPANT: 'Absolutely! I wouldn't miss is for the world. You think **Aloysius** and **Fancy** will marry then?'

WIZARD 37: 'Oh aye. **Sewn on**, from what **Queen Bee** tells me. They can't wait to be married; they are **besotted** with each other.'

RUMPANT: 'Ah, young love.'

WIZARD 37: 'Aye, young love.'

They both gazed **wistfully** out into the distance.

QED: 'Ee aw, aw aw, aw aw, aw aw.'

QED could not speak as such, but he 'ee-aw'd in **morse code**. They laughed at that.

———————

After three days of steady trekking, **Professor Rumpant Pustule** and **QED** descended beneath the cloud base that covers the Silothan mountains, into bright sunshine. Before them stretched the coastal plain and the beautiful Silvian Sea. It was a marvellous sight, but **Rumpant** wasn't happy.

RUMPANT: 'Oh no. They've done it again!'

He was referring to Fartigen University. He should have been ableto see it quite clearly, but it wasn't there. The wizard students had made it disappear. It was their party trick. They loved doing it. They thought it was hilarious. But it got on everyone else's nerves. How would you like it if your house kept disappearing?

QED could see the university quite clearly. You can't **pull the wool over** a donkey's eyes; they are too smart.

QED: 'Aw aw, ee aw ee aw ee aw aw aw ee ee ee eee aw aw ee.'

Morse code in 'ee-aw's for 'I can see it.'

RUMPANT: 'Well that's something,' **QED**. I'll follow you then.'

Fartigen University was the oldest university on **Spug**. It was set up originally to train wizards but they did all sorts of things now, from **anthropology** to hairdressing; zoology to knitting. You name it, and Fartigen University did it. It was affectionately known as '**Old Fart**'.

It took a long time to train a wizard – about a hundred years. There was a lot to learn. There was no maximum. Some students never left **Old Fart** – it was a **cushy number**.

Rumpant wanted to study **The Bonz**, but he didn't know which course to enrol on. **The Bonz** were brown furry animals; rodents, he would class them as. They looked like overgrown guinea pigs, but they had many of the **characteristics** of humans: they talked like humans, they lived in family groups. They were an organised society. They shared human emotions of love, happiness, fear, hate. They had a sense of humour. They spoke English, but they did live in burrows underground; a very un-human thing to do. Or was it? He remembered reading in the National Geographic about a tribe in Gingangooly Land who lived underground. They were human.

Zoology was the study of animals, but it was **The Bonz's** human **characteristics** that interested him most. Could **The Bonz** be classed as a human sub-species? **Anthropology** was the study of humans as animals. Could he apply the science of

anthropology to **The Bonz?** There was only one way to find out: he enrolled on the **Anthropology** Course at Fartigen University, but he soon came unstuck.

In his first tutorial, **Rumpant broached** the subject with his tutor **Dr Marzipan**.

RUMPANT: 'I would like to study an animal called **The Bonz**, sir …'

DR MARZIPAN: 'You are on the wrong course, lad. You want zoology.'

RUMPANT: 'No, you don't understand sir.'

The Bonz have a lot of human **characteristics**. I was very lucky to witness what they call **The Bonz Conundrums**. A fascinating contest that tests physical fitness, courage, skill, and an ability to think. They can talk the same as you and I. A wizard called **Wizard 37** devised **The Bonz Conundrums**. It's a remarkable piece of **social engineering** that ensures only the most able **Bonz** becomes leader. They are one of the oldest animals on **Spug**.

DR MARZIPAN: 'You just condemned yourself out of your own mouth, **Pustule**. You called them animals. Look it up in your dictionary.'

Rumpant looked **crestfallen**. **Dr Marzipan** softened a bit and said 'Where are these ...

Bonz as you call them?'

RUMPANT: 'On the other side of the Silothan mountains, in the Red Centre. It's called The Vushy Plain.'

DR MARZIPAN: 'You've been to the Red Centre and lived to tell the tale?'

RUMPANT: 'Yeah.'

DR MARZIPAN: 'I know of two expeditions who went to the red centre. They told tales of **ferocious blizzards** in the mountains and **searing** heat on the plain. Their reports were so bad that no one has **ventured** there since. Now you are telling me that you have ben there ... on your own?!'

RUMPANT: 'I wasn't on my own, sir. I had my donkey **QED** with me.'

DR MARZIPAN: 'I fail to understand how a donkey, a beast of burden, can enable you to succeed where others have failed.'

RUMPANT: 'Ah well, **QED** is no ordinary donkey, sir. He knows his way. He can even find his way in a blizzard, though he usually heads for shelter and waits till it passes. That's in the mountains. The Vushy Plain is a bit warm, but everybody stays out of the midday sun. **QED** knows where to hole up. **The Bonz** are only on the Plain dawn and dusk. It's not too bad then.'

DR MARZIPAN: 'All right, **Pustule**. Write me an essay on this **Bonz** of yours and I'll consider it. I'm not promising anything, mind. It all seems a bit far fetched to me. How did you find this remarkable donkey, by the way?'

RUMPANT: 'He found me. I was wandering around Bortapello market, looking at things I couldn't afford, when I noticed he was following me. He seemed like a friendly chap, so I took him home and gave him something to eat. He started ee-awing. I didn't think much of it. I mean, that's what donkeys do, isn't it. I don't know why, but I told him that I was in my gap year and I wanted to go travelling. He seemed to understand what I was saying and wanted me to follow him. He led me around the streets of Fartigen, showing me places I have never seen before. You know what a rabbit warren Fartigen is, sir, but the donkey seemed to know it like the back of your hand. He led me down to the beach and, with his hoof, drew a one dimensional map of **Spug**. When he had finished, he put an' X marks the spot', exactly where Fartigen was.

It was quite remarkable. It occurred to me that if this donkey could draw a map like that, and knew exactly where he was, he would make an ideal travelling companion. That's how it came about, I just followed where **QED** led. He showed me **The Bonz**. I would never have found them on my own.

DR MARZIPAN: 'I think there is some magic going on here, **Pustule**. There usually is when you don't understand something.'

RUMPANT: 'Funny you should say that sir. When we reached the Vushy Plain, **QED** led me to this rickety old wooden cottage. It had obviously been there a long time. I had a look round and there wasn't another building to be seen. In fact, there was no other sign of human habitation at all. A grey haired old man answered the door. When he saw **QED**, he clapped his hands with delight and said: '**QED**! You're still alive! I thought the dragon had got you! How marvellous!'

QED started to ee-aw. The old man seemed to know what he was saying. He offered me his hand and said: 'Pleased to meet you, **Rumpant**. I'm

Wizard 37. Me and **QED** are old friends. Take a seat in the deck chair and I'll put the kettle on'.

He came out with two mugs of tea and a bowl of tea for **QED**. He sat down in the deck chair next to me and said: 'I expect you have some questions, **Rumpant**.'

RUMPANT: 'I do. Several. But first of all, how do you know what the donkey is saying?'

Wizard 37 smiled and said: 'Ah, **Wizard Zuron's** little secret. It's called **morse code**. I can explain how it works. It's quite simple when you get used to it.'

RUMPANT: 'Who is **Wizard Zuron**?'

WIZARD 37: 'He was **QED**'s owner. He was an explorer. Together they roamed all over **Spug**. You have probably noticed that **QED** always knows where he is. That is because **Wizard Zuron** programmed him with a Solar Alignment Territorial Navigational All Weather Vernier – or SAT NAV, for short. He's like a walking map, compass and direction finder all rolled into one. You'll never get lost when you are with **QED**.'

RUMPANT: 'I've been calling him Dave, but **QED** is obviously the name **Wizard Zuron** called him. What happened to **Wizard Zuron**?'

WIZARD 37: 'He had a massive fight with a dragon. Not any old dragon; the biggest dragon of them all: **Dragon Inferno**. **Wizard Zuron** didn't go looking for trouble. In fact, he went out of his way to avoid it. But there was one place that he wanted to explore, but he daren't because it was too dangerous. It had been eating away at him for years, until he could resist it no longer. He had to go while he still had the strength.

He told **QED** to stay behind. In fact, he insisted on it, but **QED** followed his old master anyway.

If you look on any of the old maps, you will see there is an area up to the north that says: 'THERE BE DRAGONS'. No human being has ever been here and got out alive. This is where **Wizard Zuron** went. After three days and no sign of a dragon, he relaxed a bit and even allowed **QED** to catch up with him. He knew he was following. He thought maybe it is all **superstition** and **fantasy**. Maybe there are no dragons. How wrong he was.

They met a small dragon first; only about four foot long. He eyed them warily and tried to blow out a flame from his nostrils but all he managed was a puff of smoke. **Wizard Zuron** and **QED** laughed at him. Fatal mistake. This was **Dragon Inferno's** son, **Volcanic**. They didn't know it, but they had just **thrown down the gauntlet**.

They had been travelling mostly through dense forest when they emerged, unexpectedly, into a clearing. For the first time in days, they felt the warmth of the sun.

WIZARD ZURON: 'We'll rest here a while, **QED**. Have a spot of lunch.'

They settled down and made themselves comfortable on the grass. A shadow fell over the clearing. There was the sound of large leather wings flapping and a huge Dragon settled down on the other side of the clearing. Yes, that's right. It was **Dragon Inferno**.

He raised himself up to his full height – about 20 foot – and said in a big, deep voice: 'No one laughs at my son, prepare to die, **infidel**.'

Flames leapt out of **Dragon Inferno's** nostrils and hit **Wizard Zuron** full on. But his force field held and he shot up in the air, landing on the top of one of the 60 foot high trees that surrounded the clearing. **Wizard Zuron** pointed his magic rod at the base of one of the trees. A lightning bolt leapt out of it and struck the tree. There was a loud 'CRACK' and the tree began to fall, gathering speed as it did so. It fell right across the back of **Dragon Inferno**, pinning him to the ground, which was hardly surprising as the tree weighed over 2000 pounds.

That was when **Wizard Zuron** and **QED** should have made their escape, but they couldn't take their eyes off this amazing creature. He was covered in great scales of **shimmering**, **iridescent**, turquoise, **zinging** bright lime green and blood red. He was like a giant multicoloured jewel.

Dragon Inferno let out a loud bellow, arched his back and tossed the tree to one side, as if it was just a twig. He looked around for his **adversary**. A couple of crows were dive bombing **Wizard Zuron**. He was sat right next to their nest. They were making a terrible racket. The dragon looked up at the crows and spotted **Wizard Zuron**. Flames leapt out of his nostrils as before, and the top of the tree burst into flames. The Wizard just managed to leap out of the way before the flame struck. He landed in the top of the next tree.

Wizard Zuron was worried; his force field didn't feel right. Usually, it felt like a comfortable duvet wrapped around him. Now it felt more like a string vest. It must have been damaged by the flames. He didn't think it would save him again and he dropped his magic rod. There was other magic he could conjure, of course, but he didn't have time. He was too busy leaping from tree to tree, desperately trying to keep ahead of **Dragon Inferno's** flame throwing.

A ring of fire was forming around the clearing. **Wizard Zuron** was not a young man. He was tiring. He leapt again, missed his footing, and plunged to the ground, landing with a sickening thud. **QED** was watching from behind a tree. His first instinct was to rescue his master, but what could he, a simple donkey, do against such a powerful **adversary**. The last view he had of **Wizard Zuron** was him lying, **motionless**, face down on the grass, with **Dragon Inferno** stood over him licking his lips. **QED** did the only thing he could do: he fled.

———————————

RUMPANT: 'Wow! That's quite a tale. How come you know all this if you have only just seen **QED** for the first time after it happened?'

WIZARD 37: 'Wizard **Gyromuglan** told me. He got it from the **Mitors**. They will have heard it on the **jungle telegraph**. News travels quickly in these parts. Especially bad news.

———————————

DR MARZIPAN: 'Wow! That's quite a tale.'

RUMPANT: 'That's what I said.'

DR MARZIPAN: 'Do you know what **QED** stands for?'

RUMPANT: 'No, does it stand for anything?'

DR MARZIPAN: 'Oh yes, it's Latin. It stands for 'Quod erat demonstrandum' meaning what was to be demonstrated.'

RUMPANT: 'Oh good. I'm glad we cleared that up!'

Chapter Six

After three days of steady trekking, **Professor Rumpant Pustule** and **QED** descended beneath the cloud base that covered the Silothan mountains into bright sunshine. Before them stretched the coastal plain and the beautiful blue Silvian Sea. It was a marvellous sight, but **Rumpant** wasn't happy.

RUMPANT: 'Oh no. They've done it again!'

He was referring to Fartigen University. He should have been ableto see it quite clearly, but it wasn't there. The wizard students had made it disappear. It was their party trick. They loved doing it. They thought it was hilarious. But it got on everyone else's nerves. How would you like it if your house kept disappearing?

QED could see the university quite clearly. You can't **pull the wool over** a donkey's eyes; they are too smart.

QED: 'Aw aw, ee aw ee aw ee aw aw aw ee ee ee eee aw aw ee.'

Morse code in 'ee-aw's for 'I can see it.'

RUMPANT: 'Well that's something, **QED**. I'll follow you then.'

Rumpant and **QED** walked down University Forum; there was a loud 'POP' and Fartigen University reappeared in front of them in all its glory. Actually, that's not the right way of putting it. '**Old Fart**' was not a pretty building. It was a complete mish-mash of styles. It had been extended so many times over the years, with each architect trying to outdo his predecessors. It had once been described as the architectural equivalent of a Dung Beetle! That's probably being unkind to Dung Beetles. There was: Norman Arch's Gothic Arches, flat arches, spires, domes, towers, battlements, minarets, pitched roofs, flat roofs, mansard roofs, balconies, roof gardens and countless secret passages. Fartigen University was an ugly building, but the inmates loved it. It was never boring. It was said that no one knew their way around it, but **QED begged to differ**.

Pets were not allowed on campus, but the **Governors** of **Old Fart** had a get-out clause that they used in an emergency. They classed **QED** as 'someone else's problem' so they didn't have to deal with it. Usually, it was the wizards that caused them the most problems. There were two wizard students in particular that were a **thorn in their sides**: **Dibert-Yon Longtooley** and **Shumpum Ballywater**. They were, what you might call, career students. They were in their one hundred and fourth year at **Old Fart** having failed their final exams again, for the fourth time. They had got it off to a fine art. They just managed to fail by enough to be allowed to re-take the final year, but not by too much that they were thrown off the course. The **Governors** would have liked to be rid of them, but rules were rules. The **Founding Fathers** of Fartigen University had drawn up a written **constitution**.

FARTIGEN UNIVERSITY CONSTITUTION

1. Students are entitled to re-sit a year if they fail the end of term exams by less than 13.007%.

2. No student will be forced to leave the university until they have completed the course, no matter how long it takes.

3. BOPIDES are banned.

No one was entirely sure what 'BOPIDES' were. That's what the **Founding Fathers** intended. It allowed the **Governors** to ban anything they didn't like the look of. All they had to say was: 'That is a BOPIDE. It is banned.' No one could argue against them as they didn't know what a BOPIDE was. It had proved very useful over the years. Amongst the things the **Governors** had classed as BOPIDES were:

1. The wearing of underpants outside of trousers.

2. Winkle picker shoes with sharp, metal points in the end.

3. Tapioca pudding.

This last one was surely a great service to **gastronomy**.

Both **Dibert-Yon Longtooley** and **Shumpum** Ballywater were married: **Dibert** to **Yanilow**, and **Shumpum** to **Morwenna**. **Dibert** and **Yanilow** had a daughter who they called **Thingamybob**. That wasn't her real name of course. They had been arguing about what to call her ever since she was born. She was two now, but **Dibert** and **Yanilow** were still no nearer to agreeing on a name. The poor child even answered to **Thingamybob**. She thought it WAS her name.

Shumpum and **Morwenna** also had a two year old child: a little boy called **Sputnik**. **Sputnik** was a **chip off the old block**. He loved playing practical jokes. One morning, he was digging in the garden with his little spade when a large brown worm wriggled to the surface. **Sputnik** knew that his mother was watching him from the kitchen. He picked up the worm, held it in the air, tipped his head back and dropped the worm into his open mouth. His mother screamed, dashed out of the kitchen, scooped her son up in her arms and rushed him down to the **Doctor**.

DOCTOR: 'I shouldn't worry, Mrs Ballywater, it won't do him any harm ... tell me, does he like meat?'

MORWENNA: 'Yes'

DOCTOR: 'What's his favourite type of meat?'

MORWENNA: 'Err … He seems to be keen on sausages at the moment.'

DOCTOR: 'OK, **Sputnik**. Here's the deal. It's either worms or sausages. If you eat any more worms, you can't have any more sausages.'

SPUTNIK: 'Alright. I wasn't that keen on the worm anyway.'

It's true **Sputnik** was not that keen on the worm. But he liked the reaction it produced.

———————————

Yanilow shouted to her husband through the kitchen door. It was open at the time: '**Dibert**, get your body in here this minute!'

Dibert came running in from the garden. He said: 'What is it petal soft?'

YANILOW: 'Don't you 'petal soft' me. What's that dirty great hole doing in my worktop?'

DIBERT: 'Ah … that's on account of …'

YANILOW: 'On account of what?'

DIBERT: 'On account of … I got the measurements wrong. I thought it said drill a 20 centimetre hole, but it wasn't. It should have been 20 millimetres.'

YANILOW: 'What should have been 20 millimetres? What's the hole for?'

DIBERT: 'It was supposed to be a surprise. I've bought you a 'Rubbish Gnasher'. You know how you've always wanted a Rubbish Gnasher – only it's no good now, it falls through the hole.'

YANILOW: 'Well you can't leave it like that. What are you going to do about the hole?'

DIBERT: 'I could make a feature of it.'

YANILOW: 'What sort of feature?'

DIBERT: 'How about a water feature? You've always wanted a water feature.'

YANILOW: 'There are a lot of things that I have always wanted, **Dibert**, but I do not want a water feature in the middle of my kitchen worktop!'

'WHOPP'

Thingamybob came running into the kitchen to see what was going on. She said: 'Mummy, what is Daddy doing with a saucepan on his head?'

YANILOW: 'He's wearing it for a bet.'

THINGAMYBOB: 'What bet?'

YANILOW: 'I've bet him that he can't get it off.'

———————————

After passing an uncomfortable night, **Dibert** was walking with **Shumpum** to Fartigen University the following morning, as they did every morning during term time.

SHUMPUM: 'I can't help but notice, old mate, that you are sporting an unusual form of head gear this morning.'

DIBERT: 'Too right, mate. It's from my new **Ned Kelly** Collection.'

SHUMPUM: 'Cool.'

DIBERT: 'That's one thing it ain't. It's blooming boiling in here.'

SHUMPUM: 'Take it off then.'

DIBERT: 'I can't, it's stuck.'

SHUMPUM: 'Do I detect **Yanilow's** hand in this?'

DIBERT: 'Too right, mate. She **crowned** me with it. She meant to hit me on the head with the bottom of the saucepan, but somehow it turned over in her hand and she jammed it on my head. She thinks it's hilarious – keeps calling me the **Tin Man**.' **SHUMPUM**: 'Were you arguing about names again?'

DIBERT: 'No, something completely different. She didn't like my idea for a water feature.'

SHUMPUM: 'Ah, that explains it: a water feature. Tricky things are water features. Cause no end of problems. Would you like me to remove said saucepan from your **noddle**?'

DIBERT: 'Sure would **Shumpum**, you're a mate.'

SHUMPUM: 'OK, bend over.'

Shumpum took a firm grip on the saucepan and pulled. Nothing. He took an even firmer grip and pulled again. Nothing. **Shumpum** was not one to be defeated. He blew out his cheeks and shook his arms and hands like he had seen weightlifters do. He hadn't got any **resin**, so he rubbed the palms of his hand on the gravel surface of the path to give a better grip. Then he squeezed hard on the sides of the saucepan, took a deep breath, and pulled with all his might. The saucepan didn't budge.

SHUMPUM: 'That is one stuck saucepan **Dibert**!'

DIBERT: 'Tell me about it. Am I condemned to go around with a metal **turban** on my head for the rest of my life? What about my hair? It will grow and grow but it can't get out!'

SHUMPUM: 'Chill, man. We ain't gonna solve this by brute force. We need to **put our thinking caps on**.'

———————————

Dibert and **Shumpum** were sat in class. **Wizard Pangalang** was explaining the finer points of how to cure warts when he stopped mid-sentence.

WIZARD PANGALANG: 'Will you take that stupid saucepan off your head, **Longtooley**. I can't think straight with you sat there like that.'

DIBERT: 'I can't sir. It's stuck.'

WIZARD PANGALANG: 'What do you mean, it's stuck?'

DIBERT: 'As in I can't get it off, sir.'

SHUMPUM: 'It's true, sir. I've given it a right good pull and I can't shift it.'

WIZARD PANGALANG: 'And how did you manage to get yourself into this **parlous** state, **Longtooley**?'

DIBERT: 'Well, I bought this Rubbish Gnasher, but made a mistake. So I suggested to **Yanilow** – she's my wife – that I turn it into a water feature, but …'

Wizard Pangalang held up his hand and said: 'No, don't tell me anymore. I don't want to hear about your **domestic machinations**. Go and see **Mrs Bridges** in Cooking. Saucepans are her **province**.'

Shumpum knocked on the door of 'Cooking'.

MRS BRIDGES: 'Come.'

SHUMPUM: 'Sorry to disturb you, **Mrs Bridges**, but we wondered if you could help us.'

MRS BRIDGES: 'Me? Help you? How could I, a simple cook, help a wizard.'

SHUMPUM: 'Student wizard.'

MRS BRIDGES: '**Shumpum**, you've been here longer than I have!'

SHUMPUM: 'That's true.'

MRS BRIDGES: 'I will probably regret saying this, but go on, tell me what your problem is.'

SHUMPUM: 'Well, it concerns my mate, **Dibert**, here.'

The boys stepped into the classroom. The class laughed. The boys blushed bright red. Well it was a classroom full of teenage girls.

MRS BRIDGES: 'I take it it's the saucepan on **Dibert's** head that you are referring to?'

SHUMPUM: 'Yes, it is.'

MRS BRIDGES: 'I won't ask how it got there. You can tell me later. I've got a class to teach. I take it the saucepan is stuck or you wouldn't be here?'

DIBERT: 'Spot on, **Mrs Bridges**.'

MRS BRIDGES: 'Any ideas, girls?'

GRISELDA: 'We need to apply heat to the pan so that it expands.'

MRS BRIDGES: 'Good thinking, **Griselda**. Anyone else?'

CLOIS: 'Could we stand him on his head on the cooker?' The girls laughed at that.

MRS BRIDGES: 'I see where you are coming from **Clois**. Light the gas ring and invert him. But I think that would make things worse, don't you? The weight of his body would sink him further into the pan. Very funny though. I'd like to see it.'

DIBERT: 'Don't mind me.'

BALLYWIN: 'We need to get some hot water inside the saucepan. Could we drill a hole in it?'

QUENLYN: 'Yeah, boil a kettle and pour the hot water in through a funnel.'

ROSILEA: 'Wouldn't that scold his head?'

QUENLYN: 'I guess so, but **needs must**.'

ROSILEA: 'I don't think we should do that, **Quenlyn**.'

DIBERT: 'Thank you for that kind thought, **Rosilea**.'

GRISELDA: 'What about a blow torch? Heat the pan like we do with a crème brulee.'

MRS BRIDGES: 'Ah yes, I think that would work, **Griselda**.'

DIBERT: 'I don't fancy being a human crème brulee.'

GRISELDA: 'Shut up, **wuss**. We are trying to help you here.'

DIBERT: 'Sorry I spoke.'

MRS BRIDGES: 'Right **Shumpum**. Grab hold of the side of the pan. As soon as you feel it give, lift it off sharpish. OK **Griselda**, fire up the blow torch.'

Griselda pointed the blow torch at the base of the saucepan.

DIBERT: 'It's getting a bit hot in here.'

GIRLS: 'Shut up **wuss**!'

SHUMPUM: 'Whoa'

He lifted off the saucepan from **Dibert**'s head.

DIBERT: 'Thank God for that.'

MRS BRIDGES: 'It's **Griselda** you need to thank. It was her idea.'

DIBERT: 'Thank you **Griselda**. If there is ever anything I can do to help you, don't hesitate to ask me.'

MRS BRIDGES: 'Take him up on his offer, **Griselda**. Wizards can be very useful. He says that he is just a student, but he knows more magic than a lot of wizards round here.'

Griselda shrugged and said: 'I didn't do much.'

DIBERT: 'Your modesty **becomes you**, dear lady. You are indeed a 'Dame of the First Water.'

GRISELDA:'What's a Dame of the First Water?'

DIBERT: 'It's the highest **accolade** known to man ... Or woman.'

He moved his right hand up and down, very quickly, snapped his fingers and said the magic word: '**Abracadabra**'. There was a 'CRACK' and a puff of smoke. **Dibert** opened his hand to reveal a gold medal, that he handed to **Griselda**. It was engraved:

DAME OF THE

GRISELDA

FIRST WATER

Griselda looked at **Dibert** with wide eyes and said, 'Golly!'

Chapter Seven

THINGAMYBOB: 'Mummy, can I choose my own name?'

Yanilow sighed deeply and said: 'I am sorry **Thingamybob**; we've failed you haven't we. Me and your Dad, all this **bickering** about names. It's ridiculous that you are two years old and still haven't got a proper name. Yes, of course you can choose your own name, darling. It's about the only way you are going to get one. What would you like to be called?'

THINGAMYBOB: 'Oxana.'

YANILOW: 'Mmm, that's one we hadn't considered. Why do you want to be called that?'

THINGAMYBOB: 'One of the big girls is called **Oxana**. She's ever so pretty.'

YANILOW: 'Oh well, if she's ever so pretty, that settles it. **Oxana**, it is.'

OXANA: 'What about Daddy?'

YANILOW: 'If he disagrees, we'll jump on him and tickle him until he gives in.' They both laughed at that.

DIBERT: 'Honey, I'm home!'

YANILOW: 'Hallo love. Had a good day?'

DIBERT: 'So-so. What's for dinner?'

YANILOW: 'Toad in the hole.'

DIBERT: 'Yum, yum. My favourite.'

YANILOW: '**Thingamybob** has something to tell you.'

DIBERT: 'Oh yes? What is it **Thingamybob**?'

THINGAMYBOB: 'I don't want to be called **Thingamybob** anymore. I want to be called **Oxana**.'

DIBERT: 'Oh I don't know about that. It sounds like … Ah, gerroff … Stop it! Ha ha ha ha ha. No, don't! Not there – ha ha ha ha ha.'

Yes, that's right. They had jumped him, wrestled him to the ground and were tickling him on his tummy, feet, arm pits; everywhere really.

OXANA:'Do you give in, Daddy?'

DIBERT: 'Yes, yes. I give in.'

YANILOW: 'So you agree that **Thingamybob** can be called **Oxana**?'

DIBERT: 'Ha ha ha, stop it. My stomach's aching … Yes! She can be called **Oxana**. Will you please stop?'

They stopped.

YANILOW: 'What is it you were going to say **Oxana** sounds like?'

DIBERT: 'I've completely forgotten … You know, we could have set an important **precedent** here. It's ridiculous that parents are forced to choose a name for their child when it is only a few weeks old. They have no idea what the child is going to turn out to be. I know of no other decision of such **magnitude** as choosing a name that the child will use for the rest of her life, that is based on such a **paucity** of information.

Parents quite literally pluck a name out of the air. It is just a **whim**, a **fancy**, a name they have heard on the TV or the radio, their favourite pop star, film star, footballer. It could be the name of a relative, or a friend or just a name they heard on the bus. Once your parents have chosen your name, that's it. You are stuck with it. You can change your name by **deed poll**, but it's a right **palaver**. Most people can't be bothered with it unless your name is **Reg Dwight** or **Norma Jean**.

I think there is a case for parents to give their child a 'birth name'. The child would be free to choose her own name when she was old enough to make a choice, as **Oxana** has done. All you need is an extra box on the birth certificate: one that records the 'birth name' and another that records the 'chosen name'. Once a child has chosen her name, all she has to do is go down to the Registrar, tell him what her 'chosen name' is and he will enter it onto her birth certificate. **Bob's your uncle**. It's as simple as that.

Take my name, for example. Who in their right mind would call themselves **Dibert**- Yon?!'

YANILOW: 'I have wondered, but I didn't like to say.'

DIBERT:'It was my father's fault. He said it was the name of a character in a book that he was reading at the time. He thought having a **double barrelled** name would make me more distinctive.

My mother said he caught her at a **low ebb**. She couldn't have cared less whether she lived or died, after I was born. Names were the least of her problems.'

YANILOW: 'Sounds like **post-natal depression**.'

DIBERT: 'Yes, I think it was, but it was never diagnosed. The Doctor just said: 'Pull yourself together, woman. You've got another mouth to feed.'

YANILOW: 'That's terrible!'

DIBERT: 'Yes, it is, but people didn't know any better in those days.'

YANILOW: 'You know, I think you are onto something here **Dibert**. In fact, the more I think about it, the more it becomes the blindingly obvious thing to do. Why hasn't anyone thought of it before?

DIBERT: 'That's how you can tell whether an idea is good or not. If it's good, it has a familiarity about it, even though you have only just thought about it. And, as you say, you can't understand why nobody has thought of it before.'

YANILOW: 'That is a very intelligent conversation we have just had, **Dibert**. I have always suspected that there is a sharp brain underneath that mop of unruly hair, but you **keep your light hidden under a bushel**. You are wasted at that university. It's time you graduated and got yourself a proper job.

DIBERT: 'Funny you should say that. **Old Grump** had me and **Shumpum** in to see him today. He says he has two vacancies for wizards.'

Old Grump is **Chief Wizard Ariwold Grumptilian III**, head of **The Council of Wizards** and Chancellor of Fartigen University. A very important man, but you wouldn't think so to look at him. He looked more like a tramp He hated spending money, especially on clothes.

DIBERT: 'Have you heard of an animal called **The Bonz**?

YANILOW: 'The Bonz? What a funny name! No, I've never heard of them, have you?'

DIBERT: 'No, apparently they are in need of a graduate wizard. **Old Grump** gave us a book to read. It's by **Professor Rumpant Pustule**. He's an **anthropologist** at **Old Fart**. He's studied them as a human sub-species because that's what he says they are, even though they look like a large rodent.'

YANILOW: 'A large rodent? You are not making this up are you, **Dibert**? It's not another of your practical jokes is it?'

DIBERT: 'No, look, there's the book. See? It does look like a rodent.'

YANILOW: 'I'm not sure about this, **Dibert**.'

DIBERT: '**Old Grump** says there is no pressure. Just read the book and let him know what we think. If we are interested, he will arrange a meeting with this **Professor Rumpant Pustule**.'

YANILOW: 'I'm surprised that these **Bonz** need two wizards.'

DIBERT: 'They don't. They only need the one. The other wizard is for something else. **Old Grump** didn't say much about it. Just that it's in the same area.'

YANILOW: 'And where is this area?'

DIBERT: 'It's a place called The Vushy Plain, in the Red Centre.'

YANILOW: 'THE RED CENTRE?'

DIBERT: 'I know. That's what I thought. Apparently it's not as bad as it's been painted.'

YANILOW: 'That's not saying much … I'm not sure about this, **Dibert**.'

DIBERT: 'Look love, we don't have to do anything. Let's just keep an open mind and read the book. You never know, we may just like it.'

YANILOW: '**Pigs might fly!**'

I need to describe the events that preceded this conversation between **Dibert** and **Yanilow**. It started the night before the **Bonz Conundrums**.

Wizard Gyromuglan was staying with **Wizard 37** during **The Conundrums**. They had had a few beers and were getting **maudlin**, talking about death. Not surprising really; they had both turned 2000 years old. Wizards live a long time but they are not **immortal**. It was a subject they had talked about before – that of finding a successor. Someone to take over when they had gone. They had tried before, without success. No one wanted to come to the Red Centre. The two expeditions that had been there had led to such bad reports about the place that no one in their right mind would consider it. But now they had **Rumpant**. Unfortunately, **Rumpant** was not a wizard, but he was a lecturer at Fartigen University: the premier university for the training of wizards. If anyone could persuade a couple of graduate wizards to take on **The Bonz** and the **Mitor, Rumpant** could. He was their best hope. He was their only hope; and he loved the Vushy Plain, didn't he. He had written a book about the Vushy Plain **Bonz**. True, it hadn't sold many copies, but a book was a book. It was there in black and white.

Wizard 37 and **Wizard Gyromuglan** decided to approach **Rumpant** over breakfast. He too was staying at **Wizard 37's** cottage, but had gone to bed some hours earlier, saying he needed an early night. He had a big day tomorrow. **Rumpant** listened to what the two wizards had to say with interest. He had often thought that **Wizard 37** in particular was growing very frail and wondered what **The Bonz** would do if anything happened to him. **Rumpant** readily agreed to make an appointment to see **Old Grump** as soon as he got back to **Old Fart**.

Professor Rumpant Pustule knocked on **Chief Wizard Ariwold Grumptilian III's** door. There was a shout from within: 'COME!'

Rumpant opened the door and said: 'Can I have a word with you sometime, sir. There is something important I would like to discuss.'

ARIWOLD: 'Well, if it's important, we best tackle it now. Sit yourself down and tell me what's troubling you.'

RUMPANT: 'Well, it's about a couple of wizards called **Wizard 37** and **Wizard Gyromuglan**.'

ARIWOLD: 'Good Lord! Are they still alive? I haven't seen them in ages. How are the old **reprobates**?'

RUMPANT: 'I think you would find them much the same, sir, but they are aware of their own **mortality**. They have asked me to approach you on the subject of recruiting a couple of graduate wizards that they can train up to take over from them.'

ARIWOLD: 'Yes, I can see where they are coming from. Mathematics is not my strong point, but, if I'm not mistaken, they must have turned 2000 by now.'

RUMPANT: 'Yes, that's right, Sir. Amazing, isn't it?'

ARIWOLD: 'Indeed. Other wizards have achieved that great age, but I can count them on the fingers of one hand. What is your connection with **Wizard 37** and **Wizard Gyromuglan**?

RUMPANT: 'I have made **The Bonz** the subject of my life's study. **Wizard 37** is **The Bonz's** wizard. I know **Wizard Gyromuglan** as **Wizard 37's** friend, but I'm not too sure what he does. The **Mitor** comes under his **auspices**, but I think there is more to him than that. He seems to be sort of Lord of the Silothan Mountains. I've no idea where he lives, only that it can't be far.'

ARIWOLD: 'Ah, yes. I can place you now: **Professor Rumpant Pustule**, isn't it. You wrote a book on **The Bonz**, didn't you. I read it. Fascinating creatures. Their behaviour is completely out of **kilter** with their looks. You must excuse me for not recognizing you sooner. Fartigen University is a big place. People coming and going all the time. It takes a bit of keeping up with.'

RUMPANT: 'Yes, I'm sure it does, sir. It's my fault anyway for not introducing myself.

ARIWOLD: 'Yes, yes. Well, never mind all that. Excuse me for being frank, **Professor Pustule**, but if my memory serves me correctly, apart from **The Bonz Conundrums**, which are a very accomplished piece of **social engineering**, **The Bonz** lead very **mundane** lives. Your book, in common with many academics, is full of facts, figures and studies that only you find interesting. I found the book **soporific**, in common with many books of its type.

RUMPANT: 'As much as it pains me, sir, I have to agree with your assessment.'

ARIWOLD: 'I think, therefore, that we are not looking for a 'top of the class' wizard here. He would just get bored and move on. Nor are we looking for a 'bottom of the class' wizard. **Wizard 37** may like a quiet life, but he is no mug.

RUMPANT: 'My thoughts exactly, sir. We need someone who is content with his own life, but able to rise to the big occasion when it is needed.'

ARIWOLD: 'Mmm, interesting. Leave it with me, **Professor Pustule**. I'm sure there is such a person.

It's just a case of drawing him out. There is a spell I could use. It's just a case of putting my hand on it.

RUMPANT: 'Thankyou, sir. I am most grateful.'

———————————

MRS BRIDGES: 'Now then, **Ariwold**, how are you, flower?'

ARIWOLD: 'All the better for seeing you, **Mrs Bridges**. What **delectations** have you brought to tickle my taste buds this evening?'

MRS BRIDGES: 'Nothing special, it's just a chicken casserole.'

ARIWOLD: 'Ah, my favourite.'

He always said that, no matter what she brought him, which was hardly surprising considering what he would have eaten, left to his own devices. **Mrs Bridges** had taken to bringing **Chief Wizard Ariwold Grumptilian III's** evening meal ever since she discovered him eating cold baked beans out of a tin with a spoon. She didn't have to do it, but she couldn't bear the thought of him neglecting himself like that. Besides, she liked the old boy.

MRS BRIDGES: 'We had a bit of excitement today in class, **Ariwold**. Two wizards came to see us.'

ARIWOLD: 'Did they now? And who were those two **presumptuous** wizards, interrupting your cookery class? They weren't there to steal your secret Yorkshire pudding recipe, were they?'

Mrs Bridges laughed and said: 'No, nothing like that. It's not so secret anyway; all the girls know it.'

ARIWOLD: 'Ah, but they are sworn to secrecy: 'The Cook's **Hippocratic oath**'!'

MRS BRIDGES: 'Sometimes, **Ariwold**, I haven't got a clue what you are talking about. Do you want me to tell you about these wizards, or not?'

ARIWOLD: 'Sorry for the interruption. **Pray, proceed**.'

MRS BRIDGES: 'They are two boys I know very well: **Dibert-Yon Longtooley** and **Shumpum Ballywater**. Dibert had a saucepan stuck on his head. I won't go into how it got there; we would be here all night. Anyway, **Griselda** managed to get it off with a blow torch. **Dibert** was so grateful he made her a 'Dame of the First Water'. He magic'd up a gold medal right in front of us. It was amazing.

The medal had **Griselda's** name written across the middle and 'Dame of the First Water' inscribed around the perimeter. I don't know if it was real gold, but it certainly looked like it. **Griselda** was stunned. We all were.

It's such a shame that no one will give those two boys a job. They are too nice for their own good. They don't stand a chance against these young **whipper snappers**. They have to keep signing on at the university as students, though I've seen them do more magic than any other wizard round here. I remember one Christmas, **Shoana**, my youngest, was looking forward to Father Christmas bringing her a Cabbage Patch Doll. She had talked of nothing else. All she had put on her list to Father Christmas was a Cabbage Patch Doll. She wasn't bothered about anything else. I'm afraid we left it a bit late to buy one. **Zack** went into town the day before Christmas Eve but the shop had sold out. He tried three other shops with the same result: there wasn't a Cabbage Patch Doll to be had in the whole of Fartigen. He must have looked desperate. The assistant told him to try **Bamleys** in London. She said they were the largest toy shop on **Spug**. If **Bamleys** hadn't got one, no one would have one. My poor husband. He was shattered when he got back, but he was determined to find **Shoana** a Cabbage Patch Doll. The following day, Christmas Eve, he got up at 6 o'clock, saddled up **Old Bessie** and set off on the long journey to London. I made him plenty of sandwiches, a slice of fruit cake and a flask of tea. It would take him over an hour to reach London. **Old Bessie** isn't the fastest of horses.

When he got to London, he made straight for **Bamleys** Toy Shop and asked for a Cabbage Patch Doll. The assistant said: 'I'm sorry, sir, but we have sold out of Cabbage Patch Dolls. **Zack's** face must have been a picture. The assistant picked up the phone, spoke into it and handed it to **Zack**. He said: 'Would you like to speak to the manager, sir? He will explain.'

The manager said he was very sorry **Zack** had had a wasted journey. **Bamleys** prided themselves on being the best toy shop on **Spug**, but there had been an unprecedented demand for Cabbage Patch Dolls. He hadn't seen anything like it since the **hoola hoop** craze. He had been in touch with the manufacturer. They were working flat out, but couldn't keep up with demand. The manager said he had placed an order for 50 more Cabbage Patch Dolls, but they wouldn't be delivered until the end of January, at the earliest.

Zack said he didn't know if they could hold out that long. The manager said: 'we do have other dolls, sir. There is a very nice one called **Cindy**. It is more expensive than the Cabbage Patch, but as a gesture of good will, I can let you have it for the same price. **Zack** thanked the manager and took him up on his offer.

Christmas morning, **Shoana** was up early. She was excited and couldn't wait to open her presents. One present in particular. Me and **Zack** kept our fingers crossed behind our backs as she ripped off the wrapping paper from the doll. She looked at it in amazement, looked at us, then back at the doll. She said: 'It's not my doll! Father Christmas has left me the wrong doll!'

Shoana burst into tears. I tried to comfort her, pointing out that it was a very nice doll, but she was **inconsolable**. We didn't know what to do. We had never seen **Shoana** so upset. She was normally such a happy child.

Shumpum came round for Christmas dinner – this was before he met **Morwenna**. Poor **Shoana** tried to put a brave face on. She loved her Uncle

Shumpum, but she couldn't, the poor mite. **Shumpum** asked her what the matter was. She said: 'Father Christmas has left me the wrong dolly. I wanted a Cabbage Patch Doll, but he has left me that one.' **Shumpum** looked at the doll and said: 'Oh. I see. Yes, it's an easy mistake to make. Father Christmas is very busy you know, **Shoana**. There isn't just you. He has lots of other children to deliver presents to. Are you sure he hasn't put your Cabbage Patch Doll down somewhere and forgotten about it? Where have you looked?' **Shoana** said: 'Just under the tree.' **Shumpum** said: 'I think we should have a good look round. It's not like Father Christmas to make a mistake. Come on, we'll have a look upstairs.'

Me and **Zack** didn't know what **Shumpum** was playing at. I didn't want him making things worse and leading **Shoana** on a **wild goose chase**. I was about to say something when he looked me in the eye, shook his head very slightly, and put his finger to his lips. So I kept quiet. **Shumpum** and **Shoana** came back down from upstairs. They hadn't found anything of course. **Shumpum** said: 'Have a look behind the settee, would you **Shoana**? I'll have a look in the cupboard under the stairs.' **Shumpum** disappeared into the cupboard. I could hear him moving about. Then he emerged with a Cabbage Patch Doll in his hand! He said: 'I've found her, **Shoana**! Father Christmas must have put her down in the cupboard whilst he was sorting his sack out.' **Shoana** squealed with delight. Her little face was a picture. She took the Cabbage Patch Doll from **Shumpum**, held her in her arms and kissed her. She said: 'Thankyou Uncle **Shumpum**! Thankyou! Thankyou! Thankyou! You are my bestest Uncle ever in all the world!'

Me and **Zack** were amazed. We couldn't believe it. There was not another Cabbage Patch Doll in the whole of **Spug**. It was impossible and it had certainly not been laid in that cupboard. I had been in an out of there all morning. I was using it as an overflow pantry for all the Christmas stuff. It was magic, **Ariwold**. Sheer magic. There's no other explanation for it. I have never seen anything like it before or since.

But **Shumpum** hadn't finished. He said: 'Now that you've got the doll that you wanted,

Shoana, what are you going to do with the doll that you don't want? **Shoana** said that she didn't know. **Shumpum** said: 'I know a little girl, less fortunate than yourself, who would love that doll. Would you like to give it to her? **Shoana** said that she would. **Shumpum** said: 'Alright, we'll go to her house this afternoon and give it to her.' **Shoana** looked me in the eye and said, 'I'm sorry, Mummy. I've behaved like a spoiled child. It's just that I've wanted a Cabbage Patch Doll for so long. I've built it up into this big thing. I'm glad Uncle **Shumpum** knows a little girl who will love **Cindy**. She is a nice doll, but she is not the Cabbage Patch Doll that I had set my heart on. I'm sorry. But that's just how I feel'.'

Tears welled up in **Mrs Bridges**' eyes. She wiped them away with a handkerchief and said: 'I'm sorry, **Ariwold**. I still get emotional when I think of it. How many four year old girls do you know who could make such a mature speech?'

ARIWOLD: 'Yes, indeed. Quite remarkable … and very **fortuitous**. I am looking for a couple of wizards with just the sort of qualities that you describe.'

Chapter Eight

MRS BRIDGES: 'Now then, **Ariwold**. How are you?'

ARIWOLD: 'All the better for seeing you, **Mrs Bridges**. What **delectations** have you brought to tickle my taste buds this evening?'

MRS BRIDGES: 'Nothing special, just a chicken curry.'

ARIWOLD: 'Ah, my favourite.'

He always said that, no matter what she brought him.

MRS BRIDGES: '**A little bird tells me** that you are having a **soiree** on Thursday.'

ARIWOLD: 'I wouldn't put it as grandly as that, **Mrs Bridges**. Just a small gathering, you know.'

MRS BRIDGES: 'What have you done about the food?'

ARIWOLD: 'Fear not, dear lady. Everything is under control. I have splashed out and bought a piece of Red Leicester and a tin of pineapple chunks.'

MRS BRIDGES: 'I think we can do a bit better than cheese and pineapple chunks on a stick, **Ariwold**!' How many people are coming to this **soiree**?'

ARIWOLD: 'Err, well, there's **Mr Longtooley** and his wife, **Mr Ballywater** and his wife, **Professor Pustule** ... I have heard rumours that **Professor Pustule** has a lady friend, but I haven't seen her.'

MRS BRIDGES: 'Oh, he has a lady friend alright. Wait till you see her. She'll blow your socks off. Is that it?

ARIWOLD: 'Yes'

MRS BRIDGES: 'I make that seven, including you.'

ARIWOLD: 'Err, yes. That would be right ... I'm intrigued by this lady friend of **Professor Pustule's**. I never had him down as a ladies' man.'

MRS BRIDGES: 'He isn't. It's a long story.'

ARIWOLD: 'I'm in no hurry.'

MRS BRIDGES: 'No, I can't tell you now. I've got to get **Zack** and **Shoana's** tea ready. I want to catch the butcher before he shuts ... Come round to our place about eight, for some supper. I'll tell you the tale then. I'm sure **Zack** and **Shoana** will be interested in it too.

ARIWOLD: 'Thank you, **Mrs Bridges**. You are indeed a 'Dame of the First Water.' He moved his right hand up and down, very quickly, snapped his fingers and said the magic word: **abracadabra**. There was a 'CRACK' and a puff of smoke. **Ariwold** opened his hand to reveal a gold medal, that he handed to **Mrs Bridges**. It was engraved.

DAME OF THE

MRS BRIDGES

FIRST WATER

MRS BRIDGES: 'Wow! It's just the same as **Griselda's!**'

ARIWOLD: 'It is indeed. I should have awarded you it a long time ago for all your meals and other kindnesses you have shown me. I can only apologise for my **tardiness**.'

MRS BRIDGES: 'You have nothing to apologise about, **Ariwold**, this is wonderful. I can't wait to show **Zack** and **Shoana**. Thank you so much.'

ARIWOLD: 'My pleasure, dear lady. Or should I say, 'Dame'!'

He was very pleased that **Dibert** had reminded him about the Ancient **Chivalric** Order of The First Water. Now he had rediscovered it, he may use it again. There were a couple of other people at the university who deserved it. It was awarded to people who had gone out of their way to help others, expecting nothing in return. **Ariwold** had been awarded a medal himself, when he was a young, newly-qualified wizard. It should be in one of his desk drawers. He began searching for it. He thought he must have lost it when he lifted up an old newspaper cutting and there it was:

GENTLEMAN OF THE

ARIWOLD

FIRST WATER

When he looked at the newspaper cutting carefully, it was all about him being awarded the medal by his father: **Ariwold Grumptilian** II.

He remembered it well. It all started with his **Aunty Parlavane**. She lived in a little village halfway between Fartigen and London, called Nether

Regions. **Ariwold** liked his **Aunty Parlavane**. She always made a fuss of him. He didn't realise that it was because she couldn't have children of her own. Wizards and witches were free to marry whoever they wanted, but if they married a human, quite often, the magic didn't work and they failed to **conceive**. That's what had happened to **Baylyn Parlavane** and her husband, **Clifford.**

The **Grumptilian** family came from a little village called Schtepps, about 30 miles north of Fartigen, on the coast. Mr and Mrs **Grumptilian** had two children, **Ariwold II** and **Baylyn**. **Baylyn** was the youngest. **Ariwold II** had left the village and taken up an important post in Fartigen. **Ariwold II** was a wizard and **Baylyn** was a witch.

Schtepps was a rural community, most of the people who lived there worked on the land. They were surrounded by woodland. All sorts of beasties lived in the woods: wolves, wild boar, and the occasional tiger. Normally, these wild animals stayed well away from the villagers, but now and again, you got a rogue one. That's what had happened with the tiger: he had killed 9 sheep, a sheepdog and badly injured a shepherd. The sheepdog had sacrificed itself protecting his mother.

In a **quirk of fate**, **Baylyn** was the only witch in the village to deal with the rogue tiger: her parents were away on a cruise and her brother was working all hours in Fartigen. It was **Baylyn's** first big test since she qualified.

It was her intention to turn the tiger into a harmless, little pussy cat. But something went wrong with the spell: instead of turning the tiger into a harmless, little pussy cat, she turned him into a giant eight foot man, with a mass of ginger hair, a big ginger beard and ginger eyes. He looked fierce. He was fierce. He licked his lips and looked around the crowd of villagers who had gathered to watch **Baylyn** perform her magic.

The villagers were shocked at the **Giant**. As one, they turned and fled. The **Giant** went after them. He **rampaged** round the village attacking everyone and anything that stood in his way. **Baylyn** desperately tried to reverse the magic, but she didn't know where she had gone wrong with the spell. Nothing she did made any difference.

The **Giant** got bored with the village and headed out on the coast road, towards Fartigen. Something had to be done before he reached the big city or he would **wreak havoc**. **Baylyn** was powerless to do anything. She was sat on the bench outside the village hall with her head in her hands, crying her eyes out.

The coast guard spotted the **Giant** running down the coast road and **semaphored** the police station on the north boundary of Fartigen. They didn't mess about. The police drew their bow and arrows and shot the **Giant**. As he lay on the road, wounded, with three arrows in him, the magic **ebbed** away and he reverted back to a tiger. The police threw a net over the tiger, hauled him onto a cart and took him off to the zoo.

That was the end of that, but **Baylyn** vowed never to practice magic again. She had completely lost her confidence. The villagers wouldn't trust her again anyway. What if the **Giant** had killed somebody. **Baylyn** went hot and cold at the thought of it.

Baylyn left Schtepps. Her parents tried to talk her round but she was **adamant**. She had to get away. She didn't know where she was going. She set out at dawn the following morning, walking. She walked right through Fartigen and kept going till she got to Nether Regions, a village 30 miles south of Fartigen. She was sat on the bench, outside the village hall, wondering what to do when a young man came and sat down beside her. He said: 'You're not from these parts, are you?'

BAYLYN: 'No.'

REVEREND CLIFFORD: 'Are you in some sort of trouble?'

BAYLYN: 'Not exactly.'

REVEREND CLIFFORD: 'Sorry. Occupational hazard. I'm a Methodist minister. I'm always on the lookout for lost souls.'

BAYLYN: 'Actually, you're not far off. I guess I am a bit of a lost soul.'

REVEREND CLIFFORD: 'I'm a good listener, if you want to talk about it.'

BAYLYN: 'I don't think you'd understand. I'm a witch.'

REVEREND CLIFFORD: 'Really? Where's your pointed hat and broomstick?'

Baylyn laughed and said: 'We don't wear them all the time.'

REVEREND CLIFFORD: 'Disappointed now.'

He pulled a face. **Baylyn** laughed again and said: 'You've made me laugh. I didn't expect that. In fact, I never thought I would laugh again.'

REVEREND CLIFFORD: 'Are you hungry?'

BAYLYN: 'Yes, I am. I haven't eaten for two days.'

REVEREND CLIFFORD: 'Come on then. I can rustle us up pasty and chips. It's not exactly cordon vegetable, but it will fill a corner.'

BAYLYN: 'Cordon vegetable?'

REVEREND CLIFFORD: 'Wait till you see it.'

————————

Baylyn and the **Reverend Clifford Parlavane** fell in love, married and **Baylyn** settled into the life of a minister's wife and forgot all about being a witch. Until a young wizard who called himself **Maga Luff** moved into the village. He had been expelled twice from other counties of **Spug** for **anti-social behaviour**, but he had not learned his lesson. I don't know why he chose Nether Regions – maybe he saw it as a **soft target**.

No one knew he was a wizard when he first arrived, but it soon became obvious. **Maga Luff** bought a small cottage and set about 'magic-ing' it up into a large **edifice** with towers, battlements, and what-have-you, modelled on ones that he had seen on Fartigen University. When he was satisfied with his creation, **Maga Luff** set about **enslaving** the villagers to his **will**. His first victim was **Mrs Pomfrett,** who he had asked to cook him a couple of meals. When **Mrs Pomfrett** asked to be paid, **Maga Luff** refused point blank and said she had to work for him for nothing. **Mrs Pomfrett** was **outraged**. It wasn't just her labour; she had paid for all the ingredients too. **Maga Luff** gave her a sickly smile and said: 'If you don't work for me for nothing, **Mrs Pomfrett**, you will regret it.'

MRS POMFRETT: 'Stuff and nonsense! Pay up or I'll set my **Stan** on you. You'll be laughing on the other side of your face if I do.'

Maga Luff said something that sounded like sizerampleuber to **Mrs Pomfrett**, whilst at the same time, turning round and round and waving his hands up and down. He stopped with his back to **Mrs Pomfrett**, pointed to his bottom and said, 'POW', very loudly. **Mrs Pomfrett** felt something move behind her. When she looked round, she saw that her bottom had grown enormously: **Maga Luff** had given her a big bum.

Mrs Pomfrett screamed. **Maga Luff** laughed and said: 'If you want to get rid of your big bum, you had better do as I say, and do my cooking.' **Mrs Pomfrett** ran all the way home.

Maga Luff's next victim was **Mr Liverwort**. **Mr Liverwort** had been cutting **Maga Luff's** grass and keeping his garden tidy for a couple of weeks. He had dropped a few hints about payment, but **Maga Luff** never responded. In the end, **Mr Liverwort** lost his temper and said: 'Pay up you tight-fisted so-and-so, or I'll give you a thick ear.' **Maga Luff** said something that sounded like: 'spondum pondlebum' to **Mr Liverwort**, whilst at the same time turning round and round and waving his hands up and down.

He stopped, pointed to **Mr Liverwort's** chest and said: 'POW!' very loudly. **Mr Liverwort** felt something move and his shirt tightened. He didn't think anything of it till he got home and his wife noticed a bulge in his chest. He took off his shirt to reveal a full pair of women's breasts! His wife screamed and said: 'they are better than mine!'

Maga Luff's response was the same as he had given to **Mrs Pomfrett**. If **Mr Liverwort** wanted rid of his breasts, he had better carry on looking after his garden.

Jenny Overmantle quite fancied **Maga Luff**. She had been out with him a few times. He would have been quite handsome if it wasn't for his big thick rubbery lips. She managed to ignore those lips, as only a woman in love can, despite the fact that it was like being kissed by a sink plunger. **Maga Luff** started asking her to do things for him: iron his shirts, wash his jumpers, but she drew the line when he asked her to clean the loo. She said: 'I'm not your skivvy, you know.'

MAGA LUFF: 'Oh yes you are, **Jenny**; if you know what's good for you.'

JENNY: 'What do you mean by that?'

Maga Luff said something that sounded like: 'sizerampleuber hair' to **Jenny**, whilst at the same time turning round and round and waving his hands up and down. He stopped, pointed to **Jenny's** beautiful, long, blond hair and said: 'POW!', very loudly. **Jenny's** hair flew up into the air and left her bald. She screamed, grabbed her hair, and ran all the way home with tears streaming down her face. As she ran, her hair started to disintegrate in her hand.

Maga Luff's response was the same as he had given **Mrs Pomfrett** and **Mr Liverwort**. If **Jenny** wanted her hair back, she would have to carry on being his skivvy.

Lastly, there was **Ronny Hardtack**. **Ronny** was an odd job man. If you needed something doing, **Ronny** was your man. He had done a few jobs for **Maga Luff**: painted his front porch, put up a curtain rail, re-laid his footpath round the back. **Ronny** hadn't been paid yet, but he was used to that; it often happened in his line of work. He wasn't worried; he had an ace card to play. **Ronny** was a very good odd job man. He seemed to be able to turn his hand to anything. When **Ronny** did a job for you, you were usually so pleased that it wasn't long before you asked him to do another one. Most people were only too pleased to pay. He kept his charges reasonable. But for those who were a bit slow, he wouldn't do any more work for them until they paid him what they owed. That usually did the trick, but for those who still refused to pay, **Ronny** had his own unique way of dealing with them. One of them was **Mr Foxley**. **Ronny** had built a new brick, garden wall for him. He had made a lovely job but **Mr Foxley** kept **prevaricating**, making all sorts of excuses as to why he couldn't pay. One morning, **Mr Foxley** went to open his front door and it wouldn't budge. He went outside to see what the matter was and where his front door should have been, there was now a brick wall. It was **Ronny's** doing, of course. He had bricked it up. It cost **Mr Foxley** twice the cost of the brick wall to demolish the brickwork and replace his front door. He always paid up promptly after that. It was quite famous in Nether Regions. Everybody knew about **Mr Foxley's** bricked up front door, which served as a reminder to **Ronny's** customers not to take advantage of his good nature.

Maga Luff had heard the story too. When he asked **Ronny** to do another job for him: build a **pergola** round the back, he was ready for him.

RONNY: 'I'll build your **pergola Maga Luff**, but first I want paying what you owe me. I make it 17 pounds, 10 shillings and six pence, cash.'

MAGA LUFF: 'I won't be paying you, **Ronny**, but I still want you to build the **pergola**. Don't try any of your stunts on me. I am more than a match for you. If you want a battle, I'll give you one.'

Ronny laughed and said: 'You don't frighten me, **Maga Luff**. I've dealt with bigger and uglier people than you.'

MAGA LUFF: 'Alright, I'll give you something to be going on with: 'piterpally untin a choo'. He turned round and round, waved his hands up and down, stopped, pointed to **Ronny's** nose, and said: 'POW!', very loudly.

Ronny sneezed, then sneezed again, and again. He couldn't stop sneezing.

RONNY: 'Ahh choo! Is that the best you can do, wizard? Ahh choo! My two year old could do … ahh choo … better. You are going to regret this. Nobody crosses **Ronny** Hardtack and gets … Ahh choo … away with it.'

The following morning, **Maga Luff** drew his curtains, but no light came through the windows. He put on his slippers and dressing gown and went outside to investigate: all of his front windows had been boarded up. **Maga Luff** fumed and said one name: '**RONNY!**'

Maga Luff stormed round the village, but couldn't find **Ronny** anywhere. Everyone stepped back inside their houses when he approached. He was passing the pub, just before twelve, when he heard the sound of laughter. He pushed open the door of the lounge bar and there was **Ronny**, surrounded by all his **cronies**, telling about how he had boarded up **Maga Luff's** front windows. They were all having a good laugh.

MAGA LUFF: 'RONNY! Get those boards off my windows and get on with building my **pergola**, or I won't be responsible for my actions.'

Ronny and his **cronies** laughed at **Maga Luff**.

RONNY: 'Ahh choo! Oh yeah, look at him. Nether Regions' answer to **Arnold Schwarzenegger** … Ahh choo … More like the poisoned dwarf!'

They all laughed at that.

Maga Luff took what looked like a thin, black torch from his pocket, turned it on and a thin, red beam shot out of it. He pointed it at **Ronny**, who immediately started scratching frantically, all over. **Maga Luff** pointed the red beam at one of the **cronies** who immediately started scratching frantically all over too. He pointed it at another, then another, with the same effect. The **cronies** realised what was happening and desperately tried to dive for cover, keeping as far away from that red beam as they could.

Now it was **Maga Luff's** turn to laugh. He looked at **Ronny** and said: 'If you and your mates want to stop scratching, you had better get started on my **pergola**, **Ronny Hardtack**. But, before that, get those boards off my windows.'

He turned and marched out of the pub. As he closed the door, he could hear raised voices.

Chapter Nine

No one in Nether Regions knew that **Baylyn** was a witch, apart from her husband, **Cliff** and he wasn't telling. But she couldn't help feeling that it was her responsibility to do something about this **Wizard** who was attacking the villagers. If not as a witch, then as a defender of her husband's parishioners.

There was no point in **Baylyn** writing to her brother and asking for help. She knew what he would say. So she decided to write to her favourite nephew, **Ariwold**.

The first thing **Ariwold** did when he received the letter from his **Aunty Baylyn**, was to show it to his Dad, who people called **Grump II**.

GRUMP II: 'Poor old **Baylyn**. I do feel sorry for her. She should be able to deal with this quite easily. It's just displacement magic he is using. All you have to do is 'turn off and reboot'. But since the tiger **debacle**, she has completely lost her confidence. She seems to have forgotten that she is a witch at all.

ARIWOLD: 'I don't mind helping her, Dad, if you show me what to do.'

GRUMP II: 'You're a credit to your old Dad, **Ariwold**. I don't know what I did to deserve a son like you. You are **generous to a fault**. The complete opposite to me. No, the magic isn't a problem. The problem is this young **Wizard Maga Luff**. Expelling him obviously hasn't had the slightest effect on his behaviour. He just moves somewhere else and starts over. We are not tackling the problem, just moving it around. He needs to be **confronted** and the only way I know of doing that is in a **duel**.'

ARIWOLD: 'A **duel**? You want me to fight in a **duel**?'

GRUMP II 'It doesn't have to be you, **Ariwold**. The proper thing to do would be to **reconvene The Grand Council of Wizards,** but that's a right **palaver** and what's more, it would take too long. We need to **nip this is in the bud**. Right now, **Maga Luff** is just having a laugh, but If he carries on like this, it could get serious.

Actually, there is another way of communicating with the **Wizards**. I was talking to **Wizard Marconi** the other night in the pub. He was telling me about his latest invention, that he called his 'Natterline'. Apparently you can talk to several

wizards at the same time using this Natterline. He says it's just like having a meeting with them, except you are all sat in your own offices. Of course, it could just have been the drink talking. You know what **Wizard Marconi** is like.'

ARIWOLD: 'No, it's true, Dad. I've seen it. It's a big black box with lots of numbers on it and flashing lights. My girlfriend, **Oceana**, showed me it. She's **Wizard Marconi's** niece. He uses her in his experiments. I went right down the bottom of the garden with this little dish thing and I could hear her voice quite clearly. It's amazing!'

GRUMP II: 'Mmm, down the bottom of the garden is one thing. The **wizards** I would like to **consult** are hundreds of miles away.'

ARIWOLD: 'Oceana says that as long as there is a clear line of sight, it doesn't seem to matter how far away you are.'

GRUMP II 'As you seem to know all about it **Ariwold**, it might be best if you approached **Wizard Marconi** on my behalf.'

ARIWOLD: 'I'll talk to **Oceana**. She can wrap her uncle round her little finger.'

Two days later, **Grump II**, **Ariwold**, **Wizard Marconi** and **Oceana** were gathered around a large table in **Grump II's** office, pouring over a large map.

WIZARD MARCONI: 'Where are these **wizards** that you want to **consult, Grump II**?'

GRUMP II: 'Well, there's **Wizard 37** and **Wizard Gyromuglan** in the Red Centre; **Wizard Boradin** in Siberia and **Wizard Fontainbleu** in the Languedoc, Pyrenees mountains.'

WIZARD MARCONI: 'I suggest we site the transmitter on the roof of the North Tower of Fartigen University. That's higher than anything else in the city.

OCEANA: 'So, what we are looking for is a clear sight from the North Tower to each of these three locations.'

She fixed a red pin on the map indicating the position of the Red Centre, Siberia and the Languedoc, Pyrenees mountains.

GRUMP II: 'Well, there are no towers in the Red Centre. I can tell you that for a fact.'

ARIWOLD: 'No, but there are the Silothan mountains. **Wizard Gyromuglan** has a lodge up there. That would give a clear sight, wouldn't it **Oceana**?'

OCEANA: 'Yes, it would. Well done **Ariwold**.'

GRUMP II: 'If it's mountains we are looking for, there are the 'Urals' in Siberia and the Pyrenees in France.'

WIZARD MARCONI: 'Excellent. All we have to do now is transport the receivers to these three locations and we are in business.'

GRUMP II: 'Won't that take a long time?'

WIZARD MARCONI: 'If we use overland mail it would. But if you are willing to pay, I could send them by 'Buzzard Air Mail' and they would be there the following day.'

GRUMP II: 'How much, **Marconi**?'

WIZARD MARCONI: 'A pound each way for each receiver.'

GRUMP II: 'Eight pounds then?'

WIZARD MARCONI: 'No, six pounds. **Wizard 37** and **Wizard Gyromuglan** could share.' **Grump II** took out his wallet, extracted two five pound notes and placed them on the table. **Wizard Marconi** reached his hand out to pick them up. **Grump II** pinned it to the table with his big fat finger and said: 'I want change, **Marconi**.'

Ariwold took a pound note out of his pocket, passed it across to **Wizard Marconi** and slid the second five pound note back to his Dad. Once again, **Ariwold** had shown his dad up.

———————————

Two days later, **Grump II**, **Ariwold**, **Wizard Marconi** and **Oceana** were gathered on the roof of the North Tower of Fartigen University. It had taken all four of them to carry the big black box transmitter up the 271 steps of the Tower. They were all puffed out, even **Oceana** and she was pretty fit.

When he had recovered his breath, **Wizard Marconi** switched on and started tuning to each receiver. **Wizard 37** and **Wizard Gyromuglan** were first, they were on button one.

WIZARD MARCONI: 'Wizard **Marconi** to **Wizard Gyromuglan** and **Wizard 37**. Do you read me? Over.'

There was a lot of crackling, then a voice said: 'Who's that? Did you hear that, **37**?' Another voice said: 'I did. I thought it sounded like **Marconi**. How did he get up here?'

WIZARD MARCONI: 'Shut up you old **duffers!** It is me, **Marconi**. I'm speaking to you through the dish receiver I sent you.'

WIZARD GYROMUGLAN:
'**Discomknockerating!**'

WIZARD 37: 'My thoughts exactly, **Gyro!**'

WIZARD MARCONI: 'Good, now we have established contact, stay by the receiver you two. I'm going to try and contact **Wizard Boradin**.'

He pressed button two on the transmitter and started tuning in. There were four red lights along the top of the transmitter. When all four were lit, that indicated that the signal was at maximum strength. **Wizard Marconi** managed three red lights, but the fourth one kept flickering on and off. He decided to try it anyway: '**Wizard Marconi** to **Wizard Boradin**. Do you read me? Over.'

There was a lot of crackling, a dog barked and growled. Then a voice said: 'Stop it, **Boris**. Put it down. Give it to me. **Boris** stop that!' More growling. 'There's a good boy. It's not going to hurt you. Hold on, **Marconi**. I'll lock him in the kitchen.'

WIZARD BORADIN: 'Sorry about that **Marconi**. I think you startled him. He couldn't understand why he could hear your voice, but couldn't see your body. So he attacked. He always does that when he doesn't understand something.'

WIZARD MARCONI: 'Well, at least it proves it's working. What type of dog is **Boris**?'

WIZARD BORADIN: 'I don't know. He's a bit of an all-sorts. But he's big. You need a big dog in the mountains. I'm afraid your receiver dish thing has a few bite marks in it now.'

WIZARD MARCONI: 'Not to worry. It was a useful test with **Boris**. I'm pleased with that. Stay by the receiver. I'm going to try and contact **Wizard Fontainbleu**.'

He pressed button three on the transmitter and started tuning in. This time, he managed to get all four red lights lit: '**Wizard Marconi** to **Wizard Fontainbleu**, do you read me? Over.'

A woman said in French: 'Bonjour Monsieur. Henri is on the toilet. Can I help you?'

WIZARD MARCONI: 'Anyone speak French?'

ARIWOLD: 'I do.'

WIZARD MARCONI: 'Speak into that grill.'

Ariwold said, in French: 'Bonjour mademoiselle. Would you mind knocking on the toilet door and telling **Wizard Fontainbleu** that **Wizard Marconi** is trying to make contact on the dish receiver.'

FRENCH WOMAN: 'Oui. Ee is 'aving trouble with the farts … Oi, Henri. The dish, it speaks to you.'

WIZARD FONTAINBLEU: 'Sorry about that, **Marconi**. Overdid it on the chilli last night.'

WIZARD MARCONI: 'Your lady friend sounds delightful.'

WIZARD FONTAINBLEU: '**Michelle**? Yeah, she is a bit **rumply**.'

WIZARD MARCONI: 'That doesn't sound like a French word.'

WIZARD FONTAINBLEU: 'It's not. It's Yorkshire. I taught in Yorkshire. Great place!'

WIZARD MARCONI: 'I take it she is not your wife?'

WIZARD FONTAINBLEU: 'What do you think?'

WIZARD MARCONI: 'Nudge, nudge. Wink, wink. Say no more!'

Wizard Fontainbleu laughed and said: 'That's very good, **Marconi**. Couldn't have put it better myself. You know you better watch out. You are in danger of becoming **witty**.'

WIZARD MARCONI: 'That would never do. I'm a serious scientist.'

They all laughed at that.

'Stay by the receiver, **Fontainbleu**. It's crunch time.'

Wizard Marconi addressed the three people in the office: 'We are about to find out whether all this has been worth it. When I throw this switch, we should all be able to talk to each other. Keep your fingers crossed.'

He threw the switch and said: '**Wizards 37, Gyromuglan, Boradin** and **Fontainbleu**: do you read me?'

They all talked at once.

WIZARD MARCONI: 'Ah, I thought that may be a problem. I suggest that we wait till one person has finished talking, say your name, then say your piece. I have with me **Wizard Grumptilian II**, his son **Ariwold** who is a newly qualified wizard and my niece, **Oceana** who has assisted me in the development of this equipment which has the working title 'Research and Development 10' or RAD10 for short.

First of all, I need to establish that you can all hear me. When I say your name, please answer 'YES'. I'll use a shorthand version of your name to speed things up.

GYRO: 'YES'

37: 'YES'

BORO: 'YES'

FONT: 'YES'

Excellent. Now we can begin. I'm going to hand you over to **Grump II**. He is the reason we are gathered here today.'

GRUMP II: 'Thank you, **Marconi**. A truly amazing piece of kit. I have called for this Extraordinary General Meeting to decide what to do with a young **renegade wizard** called **Maga**

Luff, who is terrorising a little village called Nether Regions. It's all juvenile stuff really, but it's very distressing for the people involved. For example: he has given one woman a big bum to make her cook for him for nothing; he's given a man a pair of women's breasts to make him do his garden; he has turned a girl bald to make her skivvy for him. She was his girlfriend, would you believe. The man has no **scruples**. The magic is not a problem. We can soon get rid of that. No, the problem is this character **Maga Luff**. This isn't the first time he has engaged in this type of activity. He has already been expelled from Lancashire and Yorkshire for doing much the same thing. Clearly he hasn't learned his lesson. He just moves somewhere else and starts over. We need to tackle him, confront him, defeat him, break his spirit.'

GYRO: 'You are not thinking about a **duel**, are you?'

GRUMP II: 'Yes, exactly that, **Gyro**.'

37: 'Surely you don't want one of us to fight a **duel**, **Grump II**?'

GRUMP II: 'Relax, **37**. Not one of us. It needs to be someone younger.'

ARIWOLD: 'I'll do it.'

OCEANA: 'My hero!'

GRUMP II: 'Thank you **Ariwold**. That's very good of you, but this is a democratic process. There may be other candidates. We will all vote on it.'

FONT: 'If **Ariwold** does fight the **duel**, how can you be sure he will win? This **Maga Luff Wizard** doesn't sound like a push over.'

GRUMP II: 'Good point, **Font**. I will prepare him so well he should be able to deal with anything. Plus, I will give him a back-up.'

FONT: 'You mean another wizard?'

GRUMP II: 'No, a witch.'

ARIWOLD: 'You are not thinking of **Aunty Baylyn**, are you, Dad?'

GRUMP II: 'Yes, I am.'

ARIWOLD: 'She won't do it.'

GRUMP II: 'She will if she thinks you are in danger. This might be just the thing she needs.'

BORO: 'Who is **Aunty Baylyn**?'

GRUMP II: 'She is my sister.'

BORO: 'Ah, so you are keeping it in the family.'

GRUMP II: 'You could say that – if that's what we decide.'

BORO: 'Supposing **Ariwold** does manage to defeat **Maga Luff**. What are we going to do with him?'

GRUMP II: 'Ah, yes, we are getting to the meat of the matter now. He needs to be put to work on a job that will keep him so busy, he won't have time to get up to any of these **shenanigans**.'

FONT: 'Are you thinking of placing him with one of us?'

GRUMP II:'I am, yes.'

37: 'It's no use placing him with me, he would be bored to tears.'

GYRO: 'I'm sure he would enjoy being with me in the Silothan mountains but he would not exactly be rushed off his feet.'

FONT: 'It is bad timing for me. I have just set on a young wizard. I can't just get rid of him and replace him with this **Maga Luff**. He could have me before the Employment Tribunal for unfair dismissal.'

BORO: 'I could keep him busy. In fact I could keep him very busy. Siberia is a big place. Another **wizard** would be a godsend. But no one wants to come to Siberia; it is a cold, barren place.'

GRUMP II: 'You say that **Boro**, but when I came to visit you, I had a wonderful time.'

BORO: 'Yes, it is true. The people are the saving grace of Siberia. If they take to you, they will make you very welcome. They will be your friend for life, do anything for you. They took to you **Grump II**, because you were my guest. Most people never get that far. They take one look at the place and hurry back where they came from as fast as they can.'

GRUMP II: 'In that case, we will have to make him an offer he can't refuse.'

BORO: 'Sadly, that is part of the problem. We are not rich in Siberia. I couldn't offer him much.'

GRUMP II: 'I wasn't thinking of money. I was thinking of something much more **compelling** than that.'

BORO: 'Like what?'

GRUMP II: 'Like lifting a great weight off his shoulders.'

BORO: Does he have a great weight on his shoulders?'

GRUMP II: 'Not yet, but he could have.'

BORO: 'You are talking in **riddles**, **Grump II**.'

GRUMP II: 'That's because I don't know myself yet. I need to do more research. I'm thinking of using some very old magic. Some very, very old magic, right back to the beginning of time, when Spug was first formed.

37: 'All very entertaining, I'm sure, but do we need to bother with all these **pettifogging aggrandizements**? Why don't we just take away **Maga Luff**'s magic and have done with it?'

GRUMP II: 'I did consider petitioning the **Grand Council of Wizards** and asking for that self-same thing to be done, **37**, until I talked to the Chancellor of Fartigen University, **Wizard Magnanamus**. He told me that **Maga Luff** had been a very good student; a bit **mischievous** but nothing more than high spirits. He got a good degree: First Class with Honours. **Wizard Magnanamus's** reading of the situation was that **Maga Luff** had too much time on his hands. He said what he needed was a job that he could get his teeth stuck into. One where he wouldn't have time to engage in **extracurricular activities**.'

FONT: 'What about you, **Grump II**. Couldn't you fit him in somewhere?'

GRUMP II: 'That would have been my preferred option, but, like you, **Font**, I already have an assistant. I couldn't justify another one. I can't even offer my own son a job.'

BORO: 'So that leaves me, and your mysterious weight, **Grump II**.'

GRUMP II: 'Yes, it does. Provided everyone agrees with my plan.'

They all spoke at once, but it was obvious that they all agreed with **Grump II's** plan.

GRUMP II: 'Good. We now have to decide who will challenge **Maga Luff** to a **duel**. My son **Ariwold** has volunteered. Does anyone know of any other candidate?'

FONT: 'Young **Marcel** that I have just set on could do it. But I am not sure that he would want to. This **Maga Luff** means nothing to him. He has no reason to pick a fight with him.'

GYRO: 'I think that's the **crux** of the matter. There is only one person who is **motivated** to fight a **duel** with **Maga Luff** and that's young **Ariwold**. Though I am still uncomfortable about putting the boy in harm's way.'

GRUMP II: 'I am touched by your concern for my boy, **Gyro**. Obviously I don't want to put him in harm's way either, but it is no use wrapping young **wizards** in cotton wool. We have to let them make their own way in the world. This will be good experience for **Ariwold**; but I will give you my word that he will come to no harm.'

GYRO: 'Fair enough, **Grump II**. He is your son after all. None of my business really. You said that you couldn't offer him a job. Does that mean that you are out of work **Ariwold**?'

ARIWOLD: 'Well, I am taking a bit of a holiday after graduating, but, no, I don't have a job to go onto.'

GYRO: 'We can't have that, can we. Come and work with me in the Silothan mountains.'

ARIWOLD: 'Thanks, Uncle **Gyro**. I really appreciate it.'

GYRO: 'My pleasure, dear boy. We'll have a great time. Consider it a reward for all your **sterling** work solving the **Maga Luff** problem.'

ARIWOLD: 'I've got to beat him yet.'

Chapter Ten

All the villagers from Nether Regions were gathered outside the house that they were calling **Maga Luff's** monstrosity. **Ariwold,** dressed in a splendid, star spangled, purple cloak and matching pointed hat, knocked on **Maga Luff's** front door with a gnarled, old 'wooden rod' that had been in the **Grumptilian** family for generations. He shouted: 'I, **Wizard Ariwold Grumptilian III** do challenge you, **Maga Luff** to a **duel** on the Hilly Fields at dawn on the morrow to decide your fate in the case of your disgraceful treatment of the good people of Nether Regions.

Should you wish to accept this challenge, I will take no immediate action against you. However, if you refuse, I will blow your house down.'

Maga Luff opened his door, very angry. His face **suffused** an ugly red. He shouted back: 'Who the hell do you think you are coming here shouting the odds. You are not wanted here. Go back where you come from you stupid pantomime dame, or you'll regret it.'

Ariwold took a step back, looked up and blew **Maga Luff's** chimney pots off.

MAGA LUFF: 'Right! You've done it now.'

He said something that sounded to **Ariwold** like: 'alimolyluntinear', whilst at the same time turning round and round and waving his hands up and down. He stopped, pointed to **Ariwold's** head, and said 'POW', very loudly.

Quick as a flash, **Ariwold** moved his rod up and down. It became a shield that bounced the spell back at **Maga Luff**. **Maga Luff's** ears grew to ten times their normal size.

The villagers laughed. For the first time, **Maga Luff** looked a bit unsure of himself. He said: 'Who are you?'

ARIWOLD: 'I am your **nemesis**, **Maga Luff**. Be sure to be at The Hilly Fields at dawn tomorrow, or you could find yourself on **Planet Zog**.'

No one was really sure if **Planet Zog** existed, but then again, no one wanted to find out. It was the most terrible place you could imagine. Or should I say: it was the most terrible place you could NOT imagine. The mere mention of it filled people with dread. **Maga Luff** most certainly did not want to end up on **Planet Zog**.

At dawn the following morning, there was a gathering on The Hilly Fields, the like of which had never been seen before. Villagers lined each side of the Field; about 200 of them. **Ariwold** and **Maga Luff** stood in the centre of the Field with their backs to each other.

I should explain that The Hilly Fields are not hilly at all; they are flat. They are named after a man called Mr Hill who used to own the fields. He gave them to the village. They were well used: the children used them to play football, rounders, hockey, cricket in the summer. They held sports days there, fetes, markets, all sorts of things. It was a good thing that Mr Hill did, giving the villagers those Fields, but even he could not have imagined the events that would take place there today.

At either end of the Field was a post: the one on the left was **Ariwold's** post; the one on the right was **Maga Luff's** post. These were their stations. They were free to roam all over the Fields but these posts were their base.

As the sun rose above the horizon and a milky, white light spread over the Field, the **Umpire** raised his right arm in the air and fired his gun. **Ariwold** and **Maga Luff** ran to their posts as fast as they could. **Maga Luff** got there first. He turned and hurled rocks at **Ariwold** with surprising speed and accuracy. He had an old, leather satchel round his neck that he took the rocks from. He seemed to have an inexhaustible supply of them, far more than the satchel could carry. It was a magical satchel, of course. The rocks hit **Ariwold** on the back whilst he was still running to his post. One of them hit his ear. First blood to **Maga Luff** – quite literally; **Ariwold's** ear was bleeding.

Ariwold reached his post and turned to face his opponent. He moved his rod up and down. It became a shield and was able to deflect the rest of the rocks away from him.

It is worth describing what they were both wearing: **Ariwold** was wearing his splendid, star spangled, purple cloak and matching pointed hat; but **Maga Luff** looked like he was on a Caribbean cruise: multi-coloured Hawaiian shirt, bright DayGlo orange Bermuda shorts, mirror Ray-Ban sunglasses and a black bandana, with an ostrich feather in it.

There is an old saying: 'If you can't fight, wear a big hat.' **Maga Luff** was using the same principle: he looked cool, even if he didn't feel it.

Maga Luff tired of throwing his rocks and **Ariwold** seized the opportunity to attack. He pointed his rod towards the ground and traced a circle with it. He said: 'Dante's inferno.' A ring of fire formed, about 2 foot in diameter. **Ariwold** pointed to **Maga Luff** and the ring of fire rolled towards him. **Maga Luff** tried to deflect the ring of fire. He reached into his satchel and threw all sorts of things at it: a beach towel, an inflatable rubber ring, a deck chair, a bucket and spade, a rubber duck. He had last used the satchel on his holidays in Poole; he had forgotten to take them out. The ring of fire rode over all those obstacles. There was only one thing **Maga Luff** could do: he ran over to the pond that was on the side of The Hilly Field, and jumped into it. The ring of fire followed him and the water **doused** the flames.

Maga Luff stood up to his knees in the pond. He was angry. He reached into his satchel again and finally found what he had been looking for: his own 'magic rod'. He pointed his rod to the sky and said: 'AVATOR MEGALUM!' Half of the sky darkened:

the half above **Ariwold**. **Maga Luff** was still in the sunshine. He pressed the end of the rod and a thin white beam shot out and struck the dark sky. There was a lightning flash, a clap of thunder and hailstones the size of hen's eggs came raining down. They didn't just rain on **Ariwold**; they rained on everyone at that end of the Field.

People started running for cover, but **Ariwold** stood his ground. He raised his rod in the air and converted it into an umbrella. But he wasn't as clever as he thought he was: **Maga Luff's** giant hailstones were pounding on the umbrella; it wouldn't last long.

Ariwold raised his hat and two white doves flew out. They passed from the dark sky into the bright sunshine and circled round. Everyone stood and watched the beautiful birds, including **Maga Luff**. They circled closer and closer to the dark sky and, **imperceptibly** at first, pushed it back and back and back until it disappeared.

Maga Luff was so **entranced** by the beautiful white birds, he didn't notice his opponent taking aim. **Ariwold** took a deep breath and blew a jet of air which hit **Maga Luff** in the chest, nocking him off his feet and dumped him back in the pond. Angrily,

Maga Luff climbed out of the pond. **Ariwold** blew again and put him back in the pond. He did it three times. The villagers were laughing now. **Maga Luff** was getting more and more angry and exploded out of the pond, like a racehorse from the starting gate and sped towards **Ariwold**. The **duel** was entering its second stage: hand to hand combat. **Ariwold** raced to meet his **adversary**. They met in the middle of The Hilly Field with a sickening thud and wrestled each other to the ground. **Maga Luff** was bigger than **Ariwold**. He got him in a head lock and squeezed and squeezed. **Ariwold** was having trouble breathing. **Maga Luff** may have been physically stronger than **Ariwold**, but **Ariwold** was the better wizard. He temporarily turned his head into an apple and rolled clear. He sat up, shook his apple head. It went 'POP' and returned to its normal shape.

The villagers applauded. Even **Maga Luff** was impressed. Adopting a yoga pose, called padasana, **Ariwold** pushed himself up from the floor with his hands and stretched his legs out in front of him. He was readying himself for **Maga Luff's** next attack, which he knew was coming; it did. **Maga Luff** launched himself at **Ariwold** as he sat on the ground. He was going to do a belly flop and land on top of him like a big bear. **Ariwold** pulled his knees back, pivoted upwards and as **Maga Luff** fell towards him, he shot his legs out and struck him with force in the chest. **Maga Luff** recoiled in the opposite direction and landed heavily on his back, winded, desperately trying to get his breath back.

Now it was **Ariwold's** turn. He leapt on top of **Maga Luff**, pinned him to the ground and whispered in his ear: 'Had enough, **Maga Luff**?' Struggling to breathe, **Maga Luff** hissed through his teeth: 'NEVER!' **Ariwold** turned his rod into a cricket bat and **crowned Maga Luff** with it, knocking him out cold.

When **Maga Luff** came round, at first, he didn't know where he was. He felt the top of his head. There was a bump the size of a duck's egg on it. He had only been out for about 5 or 6 minutes, but he felt decidedly groggy. His eyesight was a bit blurred. Gradually, he came to his senses and looked around. The villagers were still there, lined up on either side of the Hilly Field, but there was no sign of **Ariwold**. Then he spotted him, standing in the middle of the villagers on the right hand side. He was immaculately dressed in his splendid, star spangled purple cloak and matching pointed hat. You wouldn't think he had been in a fight. In his right hand he held a golden **trident** which he was pointing in the air. **Maga Luff** didn't notice that **Baylyn** was standing directly opposite him on the other side of the Hilly Field, also holding up a golden **trident** in the air.

Maga Luff struggled to his feet, a bit unsteadily. **Ariwold** shouted: 'Do you admit defeat, **Maga Luff**/' **Maga Luff** gathered all his remaining strength and shouted back: 'NEVER!'

Together **Ariwold** and **Baylyn** shouted: '**Genesis tuchamilabin**'. **Simultaneously**, lightning bolts shot out of their golden **tridents** and collided, a distance above **Maga Luff's** head, with a huge BANG. Gasses swirled around in a ball, reacting with each other, forming new gasses, and reacting again; each one heavier than the one before, until a solid mass of planet began to grow in the centre of the gasses. The planet grew and grew until it was about two foot in diameter. Curiously, at the bottom of the planet, were two projections that looked, for all the world, like stumpy legs.

Maga Luff was **transfixed** by this **apparition**. He couldn't take his eyes off it. Without warning, the planet dropped like a stone and landed on **Maga**

Luff's shoulders. The purpose of the two stumpy legs became clear. They allowed a space for **Maga Luff**'s head. The planet was heavy, but not as heavy as **Maga Luff** thought it would be. That's because it was a young planet. Only the outer crust had cooled and solidified. The centre was still molten rock.

The clouds parted and **Grump II's** face, three times its normal size, appeared in the sky. He said: 'You have two choices, **Maga Luff**. You can either take the journey that I have prepared for you, or you can refuse and stay as you are, doomed to roam **Spug** trying to find a way of removing the planet from your shoulders. If you take the journey that I have prepared for you, the planet will disappear from your shoulders. If you do not, it will not, no matter how hard you try.'

MAGA LUFF: 'Ecky thump! That's not much of a choice, is it?'

GRUMP II: 'It's the only choice you've got, **Maga Luff**.'

MAGA LUFF: 'What is this journey you say you've prepared?'

A rope ladder descended from the cloud. **Grump II** said: 'Climb the ladder and you'll find out.'

Maga Luff would have shrugged his shoulders, but he couldn't. The planet was sat on them.

MAGA LUFF: 'This isn't real is it. It's all magic. It could just disappear, just like that.'

GRUMP II: 'Yes, it is magic, but for you it is real. I am the only one who knows how to **de-activate** the magic and I am not going to do that if you carry on doing what you are doing.'

MAGA LUFF: 'What if I say that I will change my ways, remove the **afflictions** I have put on the villagers and become a model citizen?'

GRUMP II: 'I wouldn't believe you.'

MAGA LUFF: 'Fair enough. I wouldn't believe me either. So it's the rope ladder then.'

GRUMP II: 'Fraid so.'

As **Maga Luff** began to climb, the planet disappeared. He climbed right through the cloud and emerged into bright sunshine on the other side. Two massive **Mitors** were waiting for him. There was no sign of the big face. The **Mitors** carried a long pole between them, clutched in their massive talons. Underneath the pole was slung a hammock. The eagles indicated with their massive beaks, that he should climb into the hammock. **Maga Luff obliged**. He wasn't going to argue with all that massiveness. The **Mitors** flapped their wings and set off on their massive journey. **Maga Luff** looked around. Stretching as far as the eye could see was a white fluffy cloud, like a giant duvet. Above the cloud, the sun shined bright but **Maga Luff** was in the shade, underneath the two **Mitors**' massive wings. **Maga Luff** fell asleep, bored by mile after mile of cloud. When he woke, they were flying over water; the sea by the look of it. Dark grey and angry. The tops of the big waves were flecked with white. **Maga Luff** thought they were called white horses. Again he fell asleep, bored. When he woke, it was dark. The sky was filled with little pin pricks of light: stars. A big white moon hung in the sky. They were flying over land now. Every now and then he would see a yellow light from some of the houses. The sky started to lighten. The sun was rising on the horizon. In the distance, **Maga Luff** could see a range of mountains. The foothills leading up to the mountains were green. He could see white things moving about. 'Must be sheep', he said out loud. **Maga Luff** asked the **Mitors** if they were nearly there. They answered in their own language, which **Maga Luff** couldn't understand. He didn't speak **Mitor**. The mountain tops were covered in snow. They were a breathtaking sight. Even **Maga Luff** who wasn't known for such things, was stunned by the beauty.

This time, he didn't fall asleep. The mountains gave way to a large lake. The sun sparkled on the rippling surface. At the edge of the lake, **Maga Luff** could see a building. As they flew nearer, it got bigger and bigger, until it was very big indeed. **Maga Luff** thought it looked like a prison, with great high stone walls and battlements. The **Mitors** prepared to land. They set **Maga Luff** down in front of a massive **portcullis**. A small door in the **portcullis** opened and an old man stepped out. He walked up to **Maga Luff**, smiling broadly, and shook his hand warmly. He said: 'Welcome to my humble **abode**, **Maga Luff**. I've heard so much about you. **Wizard Magnanamus** gave you a glowing report.'

MAGA LUFF: 'I'm pleased someone does. I just seem to **put people's backs up**.'

The old man continued: 'Come inside. You must be hungry after your massive journey. My daughter has prepared something special for you.'

MAGA LUFF: 'Sorry, sir. I didn't catch your name.'

WIZARD BORADIN: 'Don't apologise dear boy. My fault. I'm always forgetting to introduce myself. I've been here that long; I assume everyone knows who I am.'

MAGA LUFF: 'Who are you?'

WIZARD BORADIN: 'There, you see. I've done it again. The name is **Boradin. Wizard Boradin.** But you can call me **Boro.**'

Boro led the way up a flight of stone steps into a large hall. At the end of the hall was a massive trestle table, groaning with food. The most beautiful girl **Maga Luff** had ever seen was stood behind the trestle table, waiting to serve him. He stared at her with his mouth open. He couldn't help it. This was the fair **Princess Samantha, Boro's** daughter; fought over by many a man, but never won.

Princess Samantha didn't just dislike **Maga Luff**; she hated him with a passion, or that's what it seemed like to the young **wizard**. **Maga Luff** didn't know what to make of her attitude. He tried to **appease** her, telling her how beautiful she was, complimenting her on her cooking, her needlework. **Princess Samantha** dismissed those **sycophantic appeasements** with **scorn**. She didn't need anyone to tell her these things. She already knew. But **Maga Luff**, being **Maga Luff**, didn't hold his tongue for long. He fought back. In fact, he gave as good as he got. Their **histrionics** could be heard all over the castle, and news of them spread far and wide.

Every morning at dawn, **Jeeves, the Butler** reported to a group of 4 horsemen that had gathered outside the castle gates, on the state of the battle between **Princess Samantha** and **Maga Luff**. Once briefed, the horsemen rode off to deliver the news to the four corners of Siberia. It was like a soap opera that they all followed **avidly**; except this wasn't acting, it was for real.

Apart from **Princess Samantha** throwing things at **Maga Luff**, their battles had all been verbal. **Maga Luff** never laid a hand on the **Princess**. If he had have done, he would have got a shock; she was a black belt in Judo. But one evening, all that changed. They were sat on the settee listening to **Cordwangle** play the **lute** when **Princess Samantha** started **ridiculing Maga Luff's** fighting **prowess**. She said he: 'couldn't fight his way out of a paper bag.' **Maga Luff** leapt on her. They fell onto the floor and rolled over and over. Then a curious thing happened. Instead of fighting, **Maga Luff** kissed **Samantha**, hard, on the lips. They kissed so hard, for so long, that their lips became numb. Finally, they both flopped onto the floor, on their backs, out of breath.

Eventually, **Samantha** said: 'that's alright then, you'll do.'

MAGA LUFF: 'What's alright then? Why will I do?'

SAMANTHA: 'You've passed the test, **Mag**. If you ask **Daddy** for my hand in marriage, I think I know what his answer will be.'

MAGA LUFF: 'Test? You mean all this was some kind of game?'

SAMANTHA: 'Not a game, no. It's too important to be called that. You have been engaged in a traditional Siberian courting ritual. I have been testing you to see if you have the strength of character to rule Siberia with me once **Daddy** retires.'

MAGA LUFF: 'A Siberian courting ritual?! You mean all men have to go through this in Siberia?'

SAMANTHA: 'Not all, just the important ones.'

MAGA LUFF: 'Well, I don't know, **Sam.** If you had said that a few weeks ago, I would have **bit your hand off**, but I don't know if I could stand much more of this fighting.'

SAMANTHA: 'There will be no more fighting from now on. We are a team. We will work together for the good of the country.'

MAGA LUFF: '**By the cringe!**'

Cordwangle couldn't wait to tell **Jeeves, The Butler.**

When **Maga Luff** disappeared into the clouds, the Nether Regions villagers clapped and cheered and paraded **Ariwold** around The Hilly Fields on their shoulders. When finally they set him back down on the ground, **Ronny** approached **Ariwold** and said:

'We are all very grateful ... Ahh choo ... To you **Ariwold**, for ridding us of that **obnoxious** ... Ahh choo ... **Wizard**. I don't mean now. You are obviously tired after your ... Ahh choo ... ordeal. But if you could see your way to ... Ahh choo ... doing something about the ... Ahh choo ... sneezing and the scratching, I would be your friend for ... Ahh choo ... Life. If you want any odd ... Ahh choo ... jobs doing, just say. I'll do them ... Ahh choo ... for nothing.

ARIWOLD: 'Yes, of course, **Ronny**. I hadn't forgotten. **Aunty Baylyn** will deal with all the **afflictions** that **Maga Luff** put on you.'

BAYLYN: 'I will?'

ARIWOLD: 'Yes, I think so, **Aunty**. You did well, helping me get rid of **Maga Luff**. You need to get your **mojo** back. This is an ideal opportunity.'

———————————

Baylyn had assembled all of **Maga Luff**'s victims in the village hall:

MRS POMFRETT: with the big bum.

MR LIVERWORT: with the women's breasts.

JENNY OVERMANTLE: with the bald head.

RONNY HARDTACK: with the sneezing and the scratching.

4 OF **RONNY'S CRONIES**: with the scratching.

They were all sat on the floor, an arm's length apart, on yoga mats. **Baylyn** was sat on a chair facing them. She had a silver pocket watch on a silver chain, suspended from her right hand.

BAYLYN: 'Right, I want you to all focus on this watch. I am going to sway it, like a **pendulum**, from side to side. Follow it with your eyes. Don't move your head. Let any other thoughts drift away. Just concentrate on the watch.'

Everyone went quiet.

BAYLYN: 'Your eyelids are becoming heavy. You feel sleepy. Don't fight it. Allow your eyelids to close. Enjoy the sleepy feeling. Your breathing is slow and regular. You feel relaxed, comfortable. All your worries have disappeared.'

One by one, each of **Maga Luff's** victims laid back on their yoga mats and slept. **Baylyn** let them lay like that for a good ten minutes. Then she said: 'In a moment, I am going to snap my fingers and you will wake up and your **affliction** will be gone.'

She snapped her fingers. There was a series of loud 'POPS'.

MRS POMFRETT: sat up and her big bum had gone.

MR LIVERWORT: sat up and his women's breasts had gone.

JENNY OVERMANTLE: sat up and her beautiful blond hair had grown back.

RONNY HARDTACK: sat up and his sneezing and itching had stopped.

RONNY'S CRONIES: sat up and their itching had stopped.

The villagers clapped and cheered. Now it was **Baylyn's** turn to be paraded about on their shoulders. They were all overjoyed at getting rid of their **afflictions** and also well pleased that they had discovered a real live witch living in Nether Regions.

The villagers nominated both **Ariwold** and **Baylyn** for the Order of the First Water. **Grump II** presented them with their medals in a ceremony on The Hilly Fields. He made **Ariwold** a Gentleman of the First Water and **Baylyn** a Dame of the First Water.

Journalist **Scoby Breezly** covered the event for the **Daily Scribbler**. He wanted to know what had happened to **Maga Luff**. He was keen to get his side of the story. But when **Ariwold** told him he was in Siberia, **his eyes glazed over. Wizard Boradin** was right: no one wanted to go to Siberia.

Chapter Eleven

Ariwold knocked on **Mrs Bridges'** door. **Shoana** answered. She said: 'Ah, you are here at last, Uncle **Ariwold**. Come on in; we've been waiting for you.'

She led the way into the lounge. As soon as he saw him, **Zack** leapt to his feet and said: '**Ariwold**! The very man!' He shook his hand **vigorously**.

'Take a seat. We can't begin to tell you how pleased we are with this gold medal: 'Dame of the First Water' that you have given **Joy**. It's well deserved. She is always helping other people and never thinks of any reward for herself. But it provides me and **Shoana** with a bit of a **dilemma**. Do we have to address **Joy** as 'Dame **Joy Bridges**' from now on?

ARIWOLD: 'You can address her any way you want, **Zack**, but she is **entitled** to use that **title**, yes.'

ZACK: 'She'll be **impossible**!'

Mrs Bridges came in carrying a massive silver tray with all the supper things on it. She said: 'You mean I'm not **impossible** already?'

ZACK: 'Alright; even more **impossible**, then.'

Mrs Bridges threw a tomato at **Zack**. It hit him on the ear.

ZACK: 'See? She's already at it!'

They all laughed at that.

ARIWOLD: 'As a matter of fact, I am a member of the Order of The First Water too. I am a 'Gentleman of the First Water'.'

MRS BRIDGES: 'Are you really **Ariwold**? You never said. How did you get that?'

ARIWOLD: 'It's a long story.'

MRS BRIDGES: 'Another long story! We could be here all night! Perhaps I should start my long story first.'

ARIWOLD: 'Yes please, **Mrs Bridges**. I must say I am most curious about **Professor Rumpant Pustule's** lady friend. He is obviously a bit of a **dark horse**.'

MRS BRIDGES: 'Right, help yourself to tea and cake and stuff and I'll begin.'

The story starts deep in the Amazonian jungle. **Tanganika** and her husband **Hippolyte** were enjoying their evening meal. **Tanganika** was a good cook. Her mother had taught her well. **Hippolyte** had caught a piene nobre fish, which **Tanganika** had baked. It was delicious; a real treat. He had also picked some red cocona berries in the forest. The berries were so delicious they just ate them as they were. It all happened so quickly; one minute they were happily chatting away; the next **Hippolyte** was doubled up in pain, retching, being sick, drenched in sweat, writhing about in agony. **Tanganika** knew straight away what it was: it was a poison. Nothing else would cause such **spasms**. One of the berries must have been poisonous, but which one? She knew that would be the first question the **Witch Doctor** would ask her. The trouble was there was none left. Whatever **Hippolyte** had eaten, he had eaten them all.

Tanganika ran to the **Witch Doctor's** hut and **implored** him to come quickly to save **Hippolyte**. But **Bremusa** could not be rushed. He made her wait until he had finished his meal before he agreed to accompany **Tanganika** to her hut. By the time they got there, **Hippolyte** was dead.

The **Witch Doctor** laid his hands on **Hippolyte's** head and face. He began to chant, swaying from side to side. He was trying to make contact with **Hippolyte's** spirit. **Hippolyte's** face that had been screwed up in agony, froze when he died, relaxed until there was no sign of the pain he had died in. His face was at peace. **Tanganika** thanked the **Witch Doctor** for doing that for her husband. She asked him what he thought **Hippolyte** had eaten.

WITCH DOCTOR: 'It could be a number of things, but my guess is strychnic. But in a way, that doesn't matter. You need to convince the Tribe that you did not poison **Hippolyte**. You have enemies, **Tanganika**. You know that.'

Tanganika sighed heavily. The **Witch Doctor** was right. There were people in The Amahuaca Tribe who would love to be rid of her. The problem was her beauty: **Tanganika** was a 6 foot 4 inch Amazonian beauty. A striking woman, with a ready smile, sparkling eyes, and an **infectious** personality. A prize for any man. But beauty is a double edged sword. It can open doors for you, give you advantages that other more plain looking people wouldn't get; but it can also cause great distress.

All the men in the Tribe admired **Tanganika**, but three of them went all the way and asked her father, **Oritha**, for her hand in marriage. **Oritha** was the Tribe's greatest warrior. He had led his men against attacks by neighbouring tribes and kept them safe for the best part of 13 years. But his lifestyle had taken its toll. He was dying. But before he died, he wanted to see his daughter married. Being a warrior, there was only one way **Oritha** could decide who would marry his daughter. They would have to fight for her.

Tanganika didn't like any of them, but she would not disobey her father. She would accept the husband he chose for her. She loved **Kleoptolene**, but he hadn't asked her father for his permission to marry her. There was no point. He was a cripple. He had been **mauled** by a leopard when he was 15. His left arm was useless and he walked with a limp. **Oritha** would not **countenance** his daughter marrying a cripple and, in any case, he wouldn't stand a chance against **Aello, Hippolyte and Penthesilea**.

They had bullied **Kleoptolene** ever since his injury. If he had been foolish enough to challenge them, they would have taken great delight in hammering him into the ground. **Tanganika** didn't like this bullying. She was only 16 but she was big for her age. She had come to **Kleoptolene's** rescue several times. **Aello, Hippolyte** and **Penthesilea,** were more than a match for **Tanganika**, but attacking her would be suicide. **Oritha** would kill them without hesitation if they so much as touched his daughter. So, when the opportunity came for them to fight for **Tanganika's** hand in marriage, they leapt at the chance to at last gain dominance over her, by becoming her husband.

The Law of the Jungle was: Survival of the Fittest. Killing was a way of life; a **mixed metaphor**, if you know what I mean.

Kleoptolene was everything the three bullies were not. He was kind sensitive, loving, funny, intelligent, but as far as **Oritha** and the rest of the Tribe were concerned, he was definitely NOT husband material. **Tanganika** and **Kleoptolene** met in secret, or at least they thought they did, but there are always plenty of eyes watching you in the jungle.

There were no weapons allowed in the contest. It was unarmed combat: a kind of 'tag' wrestling bout. But there were no rules. You could do what you want: kick, bite, gouge. **Aello** and **Hippolyte** were the first to fight. They were covered in war paint: brown lines and dots, designed to make them look like a ferocious animal, such as a jaguar; and wore only a loin cloth. Though they were friends, you wouldn't think so by the way they went at each other. They both wanted the prize, **Tanganika**. Their friendship was suspended for the **duration**.

Aello and **Hippolyte** grabbed hold of each other. Soon they were rolling around on the ground. **Aello** punched **Hippolyte** in the face. **Hippolyte** kneed **Aello** in the groin. They **simultaneously** bit each other on the shoulder. **Aello**, who was, for the moment, on top of Hippolyte, screamed in pain and pulled away. **Penthesilea** saw his chance, pushed **Hippolyte** out of the way and jumped on **Aello**, pinning his arms down. **Penthesilea** drew his head back and was about to land a head butt on **Aello** when **Aello** brought his knees up sharply into **Penthesilea's** stomach and threw him off. Very quickly, **Aello** stood up, swung his leg, and kicked **Penthesilea** in the head. **Penthesilea** wasn't knocked out, but he was dazed. He could see lots of little silver stars. These days we would say he had concussion, rush him off to hospital and give him a scan. But there are no such **niceties** in the jungle. It was just part of the fight. You shook your head and carried on. But **Penthesilea** wasn't carrying on. He was sat up trying to stop his head from spinning round.

Aello and **Hippolyte** faced each other again, but as they came together, **Hippolyte** swung his fist and punched **Aello** in the eye. He punched him so hard he broke his left eye socket. **Aello** howled in pain but **Hippolyte** showed no mercy. He went in for the kill and kicked him viciously in the stomach. **Aello** bent double, desperately trying to get his breath back. **Hippolyte** shoved him roughly onto the ground. **Penthesilea** was starting to come round. Hippolyte calmly walked over to him and kicked him in the head as he sat on the ground. This time, he was knocked unconscious. **Hippolyte** was the last man standing. **Oritha** declared him the winner. The Tribe whooped, clapped, and picked **Hippolyte** up and paraded him round the village.

When the excitement had died down, **Oritha** invited **Hippolyte** to join him in his hut.

Tanganika was waiting for them.

ORITHA: 'Congratulations, **Hippolyte**, you fought a good fight. Is there anything you want to ask me?'

HIPPOLYTE: 'Yes, sir. I would like to ask you for **Tanganika's** hand in marriage.'

ORITHA: 'I see. Do you promise to provide for my daughter, to be her protector and the father of her children?'

HIPPOLYTE: 'I do, sir, with all my strength and determination.'

ORITHA: 'Do you agree, **Tanganika**, to be **Hippolyte's** wife? To cook and keep house for him, to honour and obey him and to be the mother of his children?'

TANGANIKA: 'If that is your wish, father, then, yes, I do.'

ORITHA: 'It is my wish.'

TANGANIKA: 'Then, I do.'

ORITHA: 'In that case, you have my permission to marry.'

Four years had **elapsed** since then. **Tanganika** had not produced any children, but she and **Hippolyte** **rubbed along** reasonably well. They had their quarrels: **Hippolyte** hit **Tanganika**, but that was accepted male practice in the Tribe. **Hippolyte** was a good hunter though; they always had enough to eat, until that day when **Hippolyte** ate the poisonous berries and died.

――――――――――

WITCH DOCTOR: 'As a friend of your father, **Oritha**, I will do what I can for you **Tanganika**, but I do not just serve you, I serve the whole of the Tribe. I cannot be seen to show favouritism. If I did, my position would become **untenable**.'

TANGANIKA: 'I understand, **Bremusa**. Do you think I am in any danger?'

WITCH DOCTOR: 'Yes, I do. Very great danger. Answer me truthfully, **Tanganika**: did you poison **Hippolyte**?'

TANGANIKA: 'NO, **Bremusa**. I did not. **Hippolyte** picked the berries and put them in a bowl. I didn't touch them. We ate them straight from the bowl. I could just as easily have eaten the poisonous berries myself.'

WITCH DOCTOR: 'Mmm, that's what I thought … I will go and see **Chief Clete**. Stay here. Do not move outside your hut.'

Chief Clete had not been a friend of **Tanganika's** father, **Oritha**. In fact, they had been rivals. **Chief**

Clete did not like it that **Oritha** was more popular with the villagers than he was. Since **Hippolyte** had died, **Chief Clete** was enjoying a greater degree of popularity than he had ever done. He could quite easily have stamped out the whispering campaign against **Tanganika** that had grown since her father died. **Hippolyte** had started it when they had had a minor disagreement and **Aello** and **Penthesilea** fanned the flames. They had patched up their friendship after the fight. It had become a bit of sport to blame **Tanganika** for anything that the Tribe didn't like.

Chief Clete addressed the Amahuaca Tribe:

'A great shadow has fallen on our Tribe. One of our brave warriors has been taken from us, at a time when we need him most. Our territory, where the sun rises, is being threatened by the Hudorani Tribe. We need **Hippolyte** to defend us against them, but now he cannot. Why would the gods take **Hippolyte** from us at this time? We have made our sacrifices. We have obeyed the gods' rules. I know of no one who has offended the gods. So why are they punishing us? Unless this was not the gods' doing. Unless someone else had a hand in it. **Hippolyte** died eating berries from a bowl that he was sharing with his wife, **Tanganika**. They were alone in their hut. Did **Tanganika** have anything to do with it? She says not, but she would, wouldn't she.

I am your **chief**, your leader, but this is too serious for me to act alone. I need to know what you want me to do. Once I know your views, then I will decide what to do. Go to your huts and discuss it amongst yourselves. When you are ready, we will meet again.'

The villagers didn't need to go to their huts. **Aello** and **Penthesilea** started a chant: 'Kill **Tanganika** … Kill **Tanganika** … Kill **Tanganika** … (repeat).'

Pretty soon, the whole village was chanting it.

Witch Doctor Bremusa asked to see **Chief Clete** in his hut. He said: 'We must not kill **Tanganika** in the village. She is the daughter of our greatest warrior, **Oritha**. If we killed her, **Oritha's** spirit would take **vengeance** on us. He would bring us bad luck and release evil spirits on the village'

CHIEF CLETE: 'But if **Tanganika** did kill **Hippolyte**, the gods would not let him do that.'

WITCH DOCTOR: 'I am not convinced that she did kill him. I think it was just bad luck that he ate

---

the poisonous berries. **Tanganika** could quite easily have eaten them herself. They were sharing the same bowl.'

CHIEF CLETE: 'It is too convenient. Everyone knows that **Tanganika** didn't love **Hippolyte**. She only married him because that was what her father wanted. She loves **Kleoptolene**, though what she sees in that cripple I don't know. He can't provide for himself, let alone anybody else. What would you advise me to do, **Bremusa**?'

WITCH DOCTOR: 'Expel her from the village.'

CHIEF CLETE: 'Do you mean that once she was in the jungle, she would be fair game?'

WITCH DOCTOR: 'The Law of the Jungle is: 'Kill or be killed'. That applies to **Tanganika** as it does to any animal, human or otherwise. All I ask is that you give her a head start.'

Tanganika left the village that night, under cover of darkness. No one saw her leave. She moved quickly. She knew the Tribe's territory very well, even in the dark. **Witch Doctor Bremusa** had told her that **Chief Clete** would hold off telling the villagers of her departure for as long as he could the following day. But someone was bound to find out. All they had to do was go into her hut and they would see that she wasn't there.

When dawn broke, she was about 20 miles from the village, which sounds a lot, but the warriors would be able to move quicker than she did last night. She reckoned she had about a 4 hour start on them. **Tanganika** started to run; not an easy thing to do in the jungle with all the undergrowth, but she was a strong woman and forced her way through.

After three days and nights, **Tanganika** found herself on the edge of the Tribe's territory. She had reached the **swamp**. The Tribe never **ventured** into the **swamp**. There were crocodiles in there, piranhas with teeth like razor blades and more snakes than you could shake a stick at. In her desperation, she considered plunging into the **swamp**, but, thankfully, common sense **prevailed** and she skirted round the edge of it.

The **swamp** was an unhealthy place with millions of mosquitos. Inevitably, **Tanganika** was bitten. When **Father McKenzie** found her, she was close to death. He ordered his bearers to make a **litter** and carry her back to the Mission. The Mission was next to the mighty Amazon River. They had been there for a couple of years now, but had had limited success converting the heathen natives to Christianity. The natives didn't understand the white man's religion with its one God that you couldn't see. They preferred their own gods, but they were **canny** enough to realise that the white men had some advantages. So they didn't ignore them completely. One of these advantages was trade with the outside world and the other was medicine. **Tanganika** had been headed for the Mission when she **collapsed**.

The Mission didn't have a full time Doctor, they relied on volunteer doctors who usually did a 6 week stint as part of their training. Fortunately when **Father McKenzie** brought **Tanganika** into the Mission, a doctor had just arrived from Fartigen Hospital and was able to treat her with Halofantrine. She had malaria. The mosquitos from the **swamp** were carriers of malaria. Without the doctor's intervention, **Tanganika** would most certainly have died. And it was by no means certain that even he could save her. If she had not been a strong, fit woman, she probably wouldn't have made it, but gradually, over the course of a week, she began to improve. **Father McKenzie** and **Doctor Robertson** started to discuss what to do with her.

DR ROBERTSON: 'She can't stay here. One more bite from a malaria mosquito would finish her off. There is only so much I can do.

FATHER MCKENZIE: 'You mean get her out of the Amazon completely?'

DR ROBERTSON: 'That would be ideal, yes. Could you do that?'

FATHER MCKENZIE: 'I don't know if they told you: this Mission is run by the Cistercian Order. I am a Cistercian Monk. We have monasteries and Missions all over **Spug**. There are many places I could send this unfortunate lady, but I fear they are not suitable for such a person. Us monks take a vow of **chastity**. I'm sure it hasn't escaped your notice, that your patient is a very attractive young lady. I fear that she will be too much of a temptation for my fellow Monks.'

DR ROBERTSON: 'Yes, her beauty was the first thing that struck me. If I wasn't engaged to be married, I would be tempted to take her home with me.'

FATHER MCKENZIE: 'There is always this …'

He produced a battered old **calling card**. On one side, in beautiful **copper plate** writing was written:

WIZARD ZURON
PO BOX 1471 FARTIGEN

On the reverse, in handwriting, was written:

Thank you for your Hospitality, **Oritha**.
Write to this address if I can return the favour in any way.

DR ROBERTSON: 'As a matter of fact, I have a PO Box in Fartigen. It's the best way of ensuring your post doesn't go **astray**. I live in at the hospital, along with over a hundred other people. Post can go missing.'

FATHER MCKENZIE: 'That's something I suppose. I found the card in her pocket, but it is not addressed to this young lady. **Oritha** is a man's name. One of the natives that works for me is called **Oritha**. Going by the style of the lettering and the fading, I would say the card is older than she is.'

DR ROBERTSON: 'So it could have been a card that her father gave her.'

FATHER MCKENZIE: 'Yes.'

DR ROBERTSON: 'Wizards do live a long time. There's every chance that this **Wizard Zuron** could still be around. I think it is worth writing to him. What have we got to lose?'

FATHER MCKENZIE: 'Yes, I agree with you, **Dr Robertson**. I shall compose a letter.'

DR ROBERTSON: 'I was going to write to Orelia. I said I would write to let her know I had arrived safely. You could enclose your letter with mine. She may even be able to find **Wizard Zuron** in Fartigen.'

FATHER MCKENZIE: 'I take it Orelia is your fiancée?'

DR ROBERTSON: 'Yes, she is.' What's the post like here? It is pretty remote.'

FATHER MCKENZIE: 'We depend on the boat, but there is a service called **Buzzard** Air Mail. It's more expensive but it only takes a few days. I use it when I need to communicate with the Bishop urgently.'

DR ROBERTSON: 'Will you go halves?'

FATHER MCKENZIE: 'I think the case warrants it, yes.'

Buzzard Air Mail was **Wizard Gyromuglan's** sideline and very profitable it was too. He didn't exclusively use **buzzards**. For long distances, such as to and from the Amazon, he used **Mitors**. **Buzzards** are smaller than **Mitors** but they were very useful in the cities where they zipped around the buildings as they used to zip around the trees in the forest.

Chapter Twelve

Father McKenzie was right. **Wizard Zuron's** card was over a hundred years old. He had bought a **job lot** from a scribe in Fartigen. It worked out cheaper that way. **Wizard Zuron** had given **Oritha** his card when he was exploring the Amazon.

This was on his second visit to the Amazon. On his first visit, he had travelled up and down the Amazon river in a boat. This time, he wanted to venture into the jungle. The natives on the river tried to **dissuade** him. They said that the Tribes in the forest had a reputation for being fierce warriors. They sometimes came down to the river to fish, but they were not friendly. They hadn't hurt anyone, but they looked fierce in their war paint.

Wizard Zuron wasn't bothered about fierce warriors. In fact, he looked forward to meeting them. He was protected by his force field. He travelled light. He didn't need any porters. **QED** carried everything he needed.

They had been travelling for a couple of days in the jungle. They had heard plenty, but seen very little. **QED** stopped and started, 'ee-awing in **morse**

code. He was telling **Wizard Zuron** that they were being watched. Zuron looked around carefully, but all he could see was trees.

They carried on. All of a sudden a warrior in full tribal dress, complete with war paint, leapt out of the jungle and onto the path in front of them. He was holding a vicious looking spear, that he pointed at them. **Wizard Zuron** became his most **avuncular**:

WIZARD ZURON: 'Ah, pleased to meet you at last, old chap. Allow me to introduce myself. I am **Wizard Zuron**, and this is my faithful donkey **QED**. We are here to explore your marvellous jungle. The best I have ever seen. And I have seen a few, you know. I am a bit of an explorer, you know. You name it, and I've probably been there.'

He held his hand out for the warrior to shake. He just stared at them, like they were visitors from outer space which, I suppose, they were in a way. **Wizard Zuron** was the first white man to venture that far into the jungle. They had never seen anything like him.

Four more warriors stepped onto the path behind them and urged them forward with their spears. **Wizard Zuron** and **QED** had no option but to

SPUG – The Magic Planet

follow the warrior in front. He led them into their village; a gathering of about a dozen mud huts, thatched with leaves. They were obviously expected. The whole tribe was waiting for them, sat outside their huts, including the **Chief**, **resplendent** in his magnificent headdress and full **Chieftain** robes, but he didn't look friendly. In fact, it looked bad for the two explorers. The river natives' warnings were **well founded**. They would be lucky to get out of this alive. But **Wizard Zuron** had a trick up his sleeve. In fact, he had several.

He had spotted two old ladies sat outside their hut, **regarding** him with a **malevolent** stare, their faces creased in what looked like a **habitual** frown. **Wizard Zuron** pressed the palms of his hands together, stretched out his arms, and pointed to the two old ladies. He said: 'tutunally ubergrin', clapped his hands and the two old ladies' faces broke out into huge grins. The villagers laughed. They had never seen **Ainia** and **Deinomache** so much as smile before, let alone grin.

Wizard Zuron clicked his fingers and his magic rod appeared in his hand. He pointed it to the top of one of the tall trees that bordered the village and said: 'mooty mooty bumpen owler'. A howler

175

monkey slid down the tree, ran into the village howling and shrieking and scooted round, touching the villagers on the nose, then leaping out the way before they could grab him. He even touched the **Chief's** nose. Then he was gone, as quick as he had come.

Wizard Zuron pointed his magic rod at the ground, in the centre of the village. He pressed the end and a blue light shot out. He said: 'Psophocarpus tetragonlobus'. There was a deep rumbling underground which grew louder and louder. A massive bean stalk pierced the surface and grew and grew until it was as tall as the trees. It stopped growing and leaves sprouted from the stalk. **Wizard Zuron** clapped his hands and a massive shower of green beans rained down on the heads and shoulders of the villagers. They were very tasty beans too. The women grabbed armfuls of the beans, ran into their huts with them, and rushed back out for some more.

The fierce faces had all disappeared. Everyone was laughing and smiling now. The warrior who had stopped them on the path came up to **Wizard Zuron** and shook his hand vigorously. He said: 'Welcome to our village, **Wizard Zuron**. I am

Oritha. You will be my guest. You do good magic. Our ancestors talked about the **wizards** of **Spug**, but I thought they were just **spirits**. I didn't think they were real.'

WIZARD ZURON: 'Oh, we're real alright. There are a hundred of us all together, plus students.'

––––––––––––––––––

Oritha was proud to show **Wizard Zuron** and **QED** around his territory. He spent a lot of time with them. The problem, as always with people who lived in remote places, was how to reward them for their hospitality. Money was no use to them. There was nowhere to spend it in the jungle. For just such occasions, **Wizard Zuron** kept a supply of **Spug** Army penknives in one of the saddlebags that **QED** carried. As well as three different blades, they had: a pair of scissors, a marling spike, a file, a tin opener, a corkscrew and whistle.

Wizard Zuron gave **Oritha** a **Spug** Army penknife. He was delighted with it. Once he had worked out what it did, he couldn't put it down. **Diplomatically**, he asked for one for the **Chief**. He knew he would be jealous if he didn't get one. He may even pull rank and take **Oritha's** off him. They had been rivals ever since they were boys.

Wizard Zuron was happy to give The **Chief** a penknife and presented it to him himself, thanking him for his hospitality, though in truth, the **Chief** had kept his distance from them.

Wizard Zuron also gave **Oritha** his card and said if ever he could return the favour, write to him at this address and wherever he was in the world, it would find him.

Tanganika was three when **Wizard Zuron** and **QED** came to the village. She couldn't really remember them but she did have a memory of a giant bean stalk and some very tasty beans. Her father often told her stories about his **exploits**, but the one about the **wizard** and the **donkey** was her favourite. He had told her it so many times, she knew it off by heart, but still she asked him to tell her again. She never tired of it. She hoped and hoped that the **wizard** and the **donkey** would one day return, but they never did.

Shortly before he died, **Oritha** gave **Tanganika** the **Spug** Army penknife and **Wizard Zuron's** card, repeating what he had told him. She put them in her pocket.

After their first trip to the Red Centre when **Rumpant Pustule** had witnessed his first **Bonz Conundrums**, **QED** had explained to him how **Wizard Zuron**, whenever he explored somewhere and someone had been helpful to him, he gave them one of his cards and told them to write to him if he could return the favour. He didn't exactly get a flood of letters, more like a steady trickle, but he had given out over 50 of these cards and there was always someone who needed help.

The news of **Wizard Zuron's** death never reached many of these remote places. **Consequently,** people kept writing to him. **QED** showed **Rumpant Wizard Zuron's** PO Box in Fartigen Post Office and he decided to take it over and **honour Wizard Zuron's** promise. Most of the things he could deal with himself: a pair of goats, a machete, a replacement blade for a **Spug** Army penknife. But sometimes, magic was needed. So he called on the services of his **wizard** colleagues at Fartigen University. They were happy to help. Lecturing was all very well, but you can't beat real, live magic. Quite often, he was asked if he could do something about the weather; usually they were asking for rain. **Wizards** can magic up a storm, if they wanted to, but they could not control the weather patterns. So that's what they did: a flash of lightning, a clap of thunder and a **torrential** downpour that lasted all of 5 minutes. However, it was surprising how often proper rain followed those magic thunderstorms.

When **Rumpant** opened **Father McKenzie's** letter, he was happy to help. He wrote back straight away agreeing to take **Tanganika** in. He never explained in any of his replies that **Wizard Zuron** had died, mainly because no one was absolutely sure he had died.

Rumpant lived in a rambling old house that had been in his family for generations. He inherited it from his father. It was much too big for him, but he would never sell it. It was like his family's ancestral home. There was plenty of space to accommodate **Tanganika**. She could take one floor as her flat if she wanted to.

Tanganika, recovered from her malaria, if still a little weak, travelled to Fartigen with **Dr Robertson**, on the boat. **Rumpant** couldn't believe his eyes when he opened his door to this 6 foot 4 inch Amazonian beauty. He had every intention of treating her as the daughter he had never had. He was old enough to be her father. But **Tanganika** was not the sort of woman you could have a **platonic** relationship with. She was the sort of woman who could keep you awake all night. For the first time in his life, **Rumpant** fell in love, but for **Tanganika** it was more complicated. She didn't like the big city, the thousands of people, buildings, traffic, the constant noise, which is hardly surprising considering she had lived all her life in the depths of the Amazonian jungle. But one thing she was sure of: she had found a good man in **Rumpant**. She had never known a man treat her so well, even better than **Kleoptolene** and that was saying something. He was kind, respectful, thoughtful. He even opened doors for her, which was a new experience. There weren't many doors in the Amazon. She felt, with time, and **Rumpant**'s help, she would get used to the city. She was not in love with him yet. She had too many other things to **contend** with. But it would not be long before she was.

She didn't believe **Rumpant** when he told her he was 59 years old. If you saw your 40th birthday in the jungle, you counted yourself very lucky. **Oritha** had died when he was 36. **Tanganika** was 21 years old. She asked him how long white men lived.

RUMPANT: 'It's supposed to be three score years and ten.'

TANGANIKA: 'I don't understand. What age is that?'

RUMPANT: '70, but it varies. My father was 94 when he died.'

TANGANIKA: '94?! That's unbelievable! That's more than twice as long as we live.'

Rumpant shrugged.

TANGANIKA: 'So, you could have another 11 years, but you could have as much as 35 years.'

Rumpant shrugged again.

TANGANIKA: 'I'm more than happy with that, **Rumpant**. It's way more than in the jungle.'

Chapter Thirteen

40 years ago, **The Grand Council of Wizards** tried **Dragon Inferno** for the murder of **Wizard Zuron**, but they were unable to reach a verdict. The only eye witness they had was **QED** who communicates by ee-awing in **morse code**. They put him on the witness stand and he ee-awed for over two hours, stopping every few minutes for **Wizard 37** to provide a translation.

QED described the fight between **Dragon Inferno** and **Wizard Zuron**: **Dragon Inferno** breathing fire on **Wizard Zuron**, who shot up into the air and landed in the top of a tree. **Wizard Zuron** produced a lightning bolt which felled a tree that landed on **Dragon Inferno**, pinning him to the ground. The **dragon** cast off the tree and breathed more fire on **Wizard Zuron**, who leapt from tree to tree, trying to keep out of the way of that fire. And finally, **Wizard Zuron**, missing his footing, fell to the ground.

The Grand Council of Wizards debated the following three points.

1. Was **Wizard Zuron's** force field damaged when **Dragon Inferno** breathed fire on him?

2. Why did **Wizard Zuron** leap from tree to tree ahead of the flames and not throw some magic back at **Dragon Inferno?**

3. Did the fall kill **Wizard Zuron?**

QED testified that **Wizard Zuron** did not move after he hit the ground. Normally, falling from such a height – 60 foot – would not be a problem for a **wizard**; his force field would protect him. **The Wizards** debated backwards and forwards on the state of **Wizard Zuron's** force field. They came to the conclusion that the force field must have been damaged to some extent, otherwise he would have used it to protect himself against the flames and not leap from tree to tree to avoid them. The sixty four thousand dollar question was: How damaged was **Wizard Zuron's** force field? If it had been completely destroyed, he would not have survived the fall. But if it had been only partially operational, it would still have cushioned his fall to some extent.

The Wizards thought it unlikely that **Dragon Inferno** had completely destroyed **Wizard Zuron's** force field. Force fields are pretty robust. They have to be to do their job. So the question was: to what degree had the force field been damaged. Despite their best efforts, **The Wizards** were not able to agree on how much **Wizard Zuron's** force field had been damaged. There were two options.

A) The force field had cushioned the impact but **Wizard Zuron** had been knocked unconscious.

B) The force field was so weak, and the weight of **Wizard Zuron's** body was so great, falling from that height, it passed straight through the force field and he hit the ground with full force, which would have killed him.

QED had left **Wizard Zuron** lying on the ground with **Dragon Inferno** stood over him, licking his lips. The poor **donkey** was **distraught**. He said he felt guilty for leaving him like that, but he had just panicked and ran. **The Wizards** reassured him that there was nothing he could have done. If he had tried to rescue **Wizard Zuron**, he would have just sacrificed himself needlessly and they would never have known what had happened. At least now, they had the opportunity of bringing **Dragon Inferno** to justice. And they would have done if they knew what had happened next. The problem was there were no witnesses to what happened next. They needed to know if **Dragon Inferno**:

a) Had eaten **Wizard Zuron**

b) Incinerated him

c) Carried him off into the forest and killed him

d) Carried him off into the forest and held him captive.

The debate raged on into the night, but eventually, **The Wizards** had to accept that they were not going to be able to reach a verdict; there were just too many unknowns. But the charge would remain on the statute book and could be revived if new evidence was presented, There was no time limit. **Wizards** had long memories, but the law had an even longer memory. In fact, it never forgot, even if it took a thousand years. They would find out the truth about **Dragon Inferno** versus **Wizard Zuron**.

Which is exactly what did happen 40 years later, and from a very unexpected source.

Dragon Volcanic was a full grown **dragon** now, almost as big as his **father**, but not quite. But, in character, he couldn't have been more different. He was the kindest dragon you would ever meet. It all stemmed from that fight between **Dragon Inferno** and **Wizard Zuron**. **Dragon Volcanic** blamed himself for it and had carried the guilt ever since. If he had not told his **father** that **Wizard Zuron** had laughed at him, the fight would not have happened and **Wizard Zuron** would still be alive today.

Dragon Volcanic witnessed it all. He saw his **father** breathe fire onto **Wizard Zuron**, saw him chase him around the tree tops, breathing fire into him. He saw **Wizard Zuron** fall to the ground. He watched as his **father** picked up **Wizard Zuron** in his mouth and carried him off to his **lair** in the forest. He laid him on a stone slab and left him there, while he went and had a **nap**. Breathing fire is an exhausting business.

Dragon Volcanic persuaded his **Mother**, **Wendy**, to help him carry **Wizard Zuron** to her private quarters: a cave in a part of the forest that her husband never visited. **Dragon Inferno** may be a big, fearsome **dragon**, but in domestic matters, his wife ruled the roost. He knew better than to disturb her in her private quarters.

When **Dragon Inferno** woke to find that **Wizard Zuron** had gone, he let out an enormous bellow and **rampaged** all over the forest looking for him.

But he never thought to look in his wife, **Wendy**'s private quarters. In any case, they were **off-limits** to him. He didn't know what **Wendy** would do if he **transgressed**, but **on the other hand**, he didn't want to find out. She was a full grown dragon and could **inflict** some damage if she wanted to.

Volcanic and **Wendy** didn't know how to tell if **Wizard Zuron** was alive or dead. They had never seen a **wizard** before. They didn't know how to take his pulse, check his breathing, listen to his heart beat – but after a couple of weeks, it became, even to them, obvious that **Wizard Zuron** was not alive. **Volcanic** had found **Wizard Zuron's** magic rod, where he dropped it in the clearing, and placed it next to his body, in the hope that it may somehow revive him, but it didn't.

From that moment on, **Dragon Volcanic** changed from a ferocious **dragon** into a caring **dragon**. Rather than follow his **father's** example, and terrify all the animals in the forest, he went out of his way to help them, look after them and be their friend. The animals were so **sceptical** at first; not surprising really, a caring **dragon** was unheard of. But **Volcanic** proved his good intentions time and time again, until they had to accept that he had changed his ways. He rescued a duck stuck up a tree; he made a fox let go of a hedgehog; he stood guard whilst a family of blue tit chicks **fledged** and he started collecting wild flowers and pressing them in a book.

Dragon Inferno went **ballistic** when he heard of all these things his son was doing. He called him all the names under the sun: wimp, coward, turncoat, a disgrace to the **dragon** race. He went on and on, but he didn't strike **Volcanic**. **Wendy** said nothing in the face of this **tirade**. She just watched him intently, ready if he made a move. In the end, **Dragon Inferno** stormed off into the forest. He wanted to shake the **living daylights** out of his son, but with **Wendy** stood there, he daren't take the risk. If she breathed fire on him, he could be in big trouble.

Wendy moved **Volcanic** out of **Dragon Inferno's lair** and into her own private quarters, where she could keep an eye on him. She didn't trust her husband. He could do something when her back was turned.

And that's how it remained for the next 40 years, until a **Mitor** got blown off course on a mail run and ended up stuck in the middle of a bush in the forest.

Volcanic heard his calls and rescued him. He was in a bit of a state: he had lost quite a few feathers and it looked like his right wing was damaged.

Volcanic took the **Mitor** back to his **Mother's** quarters, gave him a couple of mice and a drink of water. He fell on it, **ravenously**. He hadn't eaten for two days. Gradually, **Volcanic** nursed the **Mitor** back to health. Fortunately his wing was OK. He would still be able to fly. As his health improved, the **Mitor** started to explore **Wendy's** quarters. He soon came upon the body of **Wizard Zuron**.

VOLCANIC: 'Ah, I see you've found him.'

MITOR: 'Is this who I think it is?'

VOLCANIC: 'It's **Wizard Zuron**. Do you know **Wizard Zuron?**'

MITOR: 'I know of him. My grandfather was the **Mitor** who first heard about the fight between **Dragon Inferno** and **Wizard Zuron**. He heard it on the Jungle Telegraph and told **Wizard Gyromuglan** – he's our boss. **Mitors** can't read or write but we do have a long tradition of storytelling. My father told me the story of **Dragon Inferno** and **Wizard Zuron's** fight, as his father had told him. I recognise **Wizard Zuron's** robes from his description, even though he is a skeleton now.'

Wizards' robes are unique to them. **Wizard Zuron's** cloak was midnight blue with silver stars on it, in three different sizes: 2 inch, 1 inch and little, tiny ones. It was as **Mitor's** father had described it to him.

VOLCANIC: 'My **father** is **Dragon Inferno**.'

The **Mitor** took a step back and said: 'Really?! Blimey! I'd better watch my step. Are you sure? You don't seem very ferocious. In fact, you've shown me nothing but kindness.'

VOLCANIC: 'That's cos it was all my fault. I've carried that guilt with me all my life.'

MITOR: 'What guilt?'

VOLCANIC: 'When I was a young **dragon**, I came across **Wizard Zuron** and his **donkey** in the forest. In my childish way, I leapt out and tried to frighten them off, like my **father** did. But I was only about four foot and far too young to produce fire. All I could manage was a puff of smoke. They laughed at me. I ran all the way home and told my **Dad**. He went mad and charged off to find **Wizard Zuron**. I followed him.'

Dad found **Wizard Zuron** in the clearing and said: 'No one laughs at my son. Prepare to die, **infidel**.' He breathed fire on the **Wizard**, who shot up in the air and landed in the top of a tree. The **Wizard** sent his own bolt of flame at a tree which landed on top of **Dad**, but he managed to shake it off and breathed more flames on **Wizard Zuron**. The **Wizard** leapt from tree to tree, trying to keep ahead of **Dad**'s flames, but he fell to the ground with a thump. **Dad** picked him up and took him to his **lair**, but while he was asleep, me and **Mum** moved him in here. He's been here ever since. I would like to return him to his family so that he could have a proper burial, but I don't know how to.'

MITOR: 'I might be able to help you there, mate. In fact, I will help you; it's the least I can do to repay you for all you've done for me. If it wasn't for you, I would be a **goner**. It's interesting what you say. I knew some of the story from my **Dad** but I didn't know what had happened to **Wizard Zuron** after he fell from the tree, and I didn't know that you had met him when you were a young **dragon**. Is that why you changed from a bad **dragon** to a good **dragon**?'

VOLCANIC: 'Yes, it is. I hated my **father**. Didn't want to be anything like him.'

MITOR: 'I can understand that, **Volcanic**, but you shouldn't blame yourself for the rest of your life for something you did when you were a kid. You couldn't have known what your **father** would do.'

VOLCANIC: 'True, but I still don't want to be like him.'

MITOR: 'And I am truly thankful for that, as are the rest of the animals in the forest, I suspect.'

VOLCANIC: 'Can you really help me get **Wizard Zuron** a proper burial?'

MITOR: 'Not me personally, but I know someone who will. I need to talk to my boss, **Wizard Gyromuglan**. He will know what to do. It will take some arranging. We need a way of communicating. In the city, they use a PO Box. I wonder if we could set up one in the forest. Do you know of a large tree we could use, preferably on the edge of the forest. I don't fancy being blown into a bush again.'

VOLCANIC: 'There's a big Monkey Puzzle tree I know of but I've no idea if it's what you are thinking of. I've no idea what a PO Box is.'

MITOR: 'Can we have a look at it?'

VOLCANIC: 'Sure. Are you up to flying? That's the easiest way of getting there.'

MITOR: 'Yeah. I think so. It will be a good test.'

Volcanic flapped his big leathery wings and took off. **Mitor** followed him. The Monkey Puzzle tree was right on the edge of the forest, perfect for what they wanted. They gathered a few branches together and fashioned a box in the top of the tree, that they could put messages in, to each other.

VOLCANIC: 'I can't just keep calling you **Mitor**; that's the name of your species. Do you have an individual name?'

MITOR: 'I do. But you wouldn't understand it. We identify each other by our call. Each of us has a different call. To anyone else, we all sound the same, but my parents can identify my call and I can identify theirs. The only other person I know who can tell us apart is **Wizard Gyromuglan**.'

VOLCANIC: 'How can I be sure my message will get to you?'

MITOR: 'Address it to **Mitor 113P**. That will find me. I can't read it, of course. I will have to get someone to read it for me. I'm hoping that you can read and write?'

VOLCANIC: 'Yes, my **Mother** taught me.'

Mitor 113P was true to his word. He told **Wizard Gyromuglan** about his rescue by **Dragon Volcanic**. He also told him about **Wizard Zuron**, how he came to be in **Wendy's** quarters and **Volcanic's** long-held desire for the wizard to be returned to his family for a proper burial.

Wizard Gyromuglan wasn't just surprised at what **Mitor 113P** told him. He was absolutely amazed!! He made an appointment to see **Wizard Ariwold Grumptilian III**, Chief Wizard and Chancellor of Fartigen University, who was also absolutely amazed. Once they had got over their shock, they agreed that **The Grand Council of Wizards** must be reconvened in light of this new evidence. **Wizard Gyromuglan** said he would arrange for two **Mitors** to fly **Wizard Zuron's** body back to Fartigen University.

Chapter Fourteen

The Wizards of **Spug** were gathered in Ye Olde **Tutuchamilabin** Hall, the oldest part of Fartigen University; 1800 years old. It stood on the site of an even older wooden building that had burned down. The magnificent Hall with its huge hammer beam roof, great baulks of oak, carved with all manner of mythical beasts, was the best building on **Spug**. **Tutuchamilabin** is the proper name of **Spug**. **Spug** is just a nickname. I don't know why they called it **Spug**. I guess they got fed up of saying **Tutuchamilabin**.

There was a great deal of chat, not surprising really. **The Wizards** had a lot of catching up to do. The last time they saw each other was 20 years ago when **Wizard Gyromuglan** had a problem with a rogue **Mitor**.

They had last tried **Dragon Inferno** 40 years ago on the murder of **Wizard Zuron**. They had been unable to reach a verdict that time, despite their best efforts. They had been told that new evidence had come to light; a new witness had come forward, but no details had been given, which inevitably led to a great deal of speculation.

Wizard Ariwold Grumptilian III and **Wizard Gyromuglan** and **Wizard 37** had had to put together some powerful magic to enable their star witness to attend the trial. Nothing like it had ever been attempted before. They were keeping their fingers crossed. There was no guarantee that they would succeed; it could all go horribly wrong.

Miss Jones, the Clerk of the Council banged her gavel and shouted: 'Quiet! All rise.' **The Wizards** rose as **Chief Wizard Ariwold Grumptilian III** entered the Hall, dressed in his full **regalia**: red cloak, trimmed with ermine and red pointed hat, covered in stars. Around his neck hung a gold chain and he carried a black magic wand with a white tip.

He sat down on his throne and addressed the **Grand Council of Wizards**: 'Fellow **wizards**: we are gathered here today to try the distressing case of the murder of one of our number: **Wizard Zuron**. As you know, this is the second time we have tried this case. New evidence has come to light which I believe will allow us to come to a satisfactory conclusion. However, I must warn you, that the witness we will call has never before been seen in

Tutuchamilabin Hall. There is no need to worry, you are perfectly safe.'

It would have been better if **Old Grump** hadn't said anything at all. By telling **The Wizards** they were perfectly safe, he immediately put them on their guard. They were expecting the worst now.

Old Grump and **Wizard Gyromuglan** pointed their magic rods at the roof. They pressed the ends of the rods and a turquoise light shone out. They said together: 'arumptilaven puttleblot'. They were both pointing their magic rods at the same spot in the centre of the roof. They drew their magic rods apart and the roof opened to reveal a clear blue sky.

The Wizards gasped. This was an 1800 year old roof we are talking about here. Some of the timbers weighed over a ton each. **The Wizards** were really worried now. **Old Grump** and **Wizard Gyromuglan** would not have gone to this much troublefor nothing. They were obviously expecting something big, but what? They didn't have long to find out.

WIZARD GYROMUGLAN: 'Call the first witness.'

A lone **Mitor** flew in through the open roof and landed on the rail that ran round the witness box. Now, a **Mitor** is a big eagle with a wing span of over ten foot, but there are two big double doors that lead into **Tutuchamilabin** Hall. He could easily have been brought in through those doors. **The Wizards** turned their eyes from the **Mitor**, back up to the sky. They watched and waited. You could have cut the atmosphere with a knife.

Wizard Gyromuglan spoke to the **Mitor**: 'State your name please.' The **Mitor** spoke in a deep voice: '**Mitor 113P**'.

WIZARD GYROMUGLAN: 'Do you promise to speak the truth, the whole truth and nothing but the truth?'

MITOR 113P: 'I do.'

Gyro addressed the Council: 'It is thanks to this remarkable **Mitor** and a quirk of fate that we are gathered here today, and have the opportunity of re-trying this case. If that had not come to pass, **Wizard Zuron**'s death would remain a mystery. In a moment, I am going to ask **Mitor 113P** to tell, in his own words, the events that led up to his discovery of **Wizard Zuron**. But it is my sad duty to have to tell you that **Wizard Zuron** is no more.

He died when he fell from the tree. In your own time, **Mitor 113P**.'

MITOR: 'I was returning from a mail delivery when a huge storm appeared from nowhere and blew me off course. I looked around for somewhere to ride out the storm, but it was too strong for me. It blew me into the depths of a forest and right into the middle of a bush. No matter how much I struggled, I couldn't get out of the bush. I would have died there if **Dragon Volcanic** had not found me. He heard my calls and, remarkably, for a **dragon** of that size, carefully made a hole in the bush and gently eased me out. I was in a right state. Half my flight feathers were gone, only two of my tail feathers remained and my right wing was at such an odd angle, I thought it was broken.

Dragon Volcanic carried me back to his cave and looked after me like a mother. He nursed me back to health. When I was stronger, I started to explore the cave. It was then I came across **Wizard Zuron**. I knew it was **Wizard Zuron** because I recognised his cloak. It was midnight blue with silver stars of three different sizes: 2 inches, 1 inch and lots of little, tiny ones. It was exactly as my father had described it. I should explain, it was my grandfather who first heard about the fight between **Wizard Zuron** and **Dragon Inferno**. It was he who told **Wizard Gyromuglan** about it. **Mitors** have a great tradition of storytelling. The story has been passed down through our family, but I have to tell you that the man I saw was a skeleton.'

WIZARD GRUMPTILIAN III: 'Thank you, **Mitor 113P**. Can I have a show of hands. All those who agree that the cloak **Mitor 113P** described was one that **Wizard Zuron** wore, please raise your right hand.'

All 100 wizards raised their right hand.

WIZARD ARIWOLD GRUMPTILIAN III: 'Carried. Continue, **Wizard Gyromuglan**.'

WIZARD GYROMUGLAN: 'Of course, the cloak alone does not prove that it was **Wizard Zuron**. **Mitor 113P** said the body was a skeleton. It could be someone else who had picked up **Wizard Zuron's** cloak. To prove who it was, I need to call the next witness.'

He looked at **Wizard Grumptilian III**, who said, in a most un-**Chief Wizard**-like way: 'Go for it, **Gyro**.'

WIZARD GYROMUGLAN: 'Call the second witness.'

A shadow fell over **Tutuchamilabin** Hall. There was the sound of large leather wings flapping and a huge **dragon** descended through the open roof and settled in the middle of the Hall. **The Wizards** gasped in shock and horror. They thought **Old Grump** and **Gyro** have brought **Dragon Inferno** himself to stand trial before them. They must be mad. He could kill them all and burn Fartigen University to the ground. They all grabbed their magic rods, ready to defend themselves and tensed up ready to make a run for it. But they couldn't run; they were **transfixed** by this amazing creature: 20 foot high, with great scales of **shimmering iridescent** turquoise **zinging** bright lime green and blood red. He was like a giant, multicoloured jewel.

The **Dragon** looked slowly around the Hall at **The Wizards** and said in a big, deep voice: 'Good afternoon, gentlemen. Allow me to introduce myself. I am **Dragon Volcanic**, son of **Dragon Inferno**.'

The Wizards let out a huge sigh of relief. It wasn't **Dragon Inferno**, thank God for that. But they were still wary; still ready to run.

WIZARD ARIWOLD GRUMPTILIAN III:

'I owe you an apology, fellow **Wizards** for springing this witness on you. Quite frankly, I didn't think I had any option. If I had told you that we were bringing a full grown **dragon** to testify before you, I doubt you would have turned up.'

The Wizards muttered in agreement.

'However, this is not an act of madness on my part. I would never take a risk with my fellow **wizards'** safety. Before I agreed that **Wizard Gyromuglan** could call **Dragon Volcanic** as a witness, I insisted that I must be satisfied that **Dragon Volcanic** does not pose a threat. To this end, **Mitor 113P** took myself and **Wizard Gyromuglan** to meet **Dragon Volcanic** in his forest. It soon became **apparent** that we were not dealing with any ordinary **dragon**. He carried a huge guilt on his shoulders that had turned him from a terrifying, fire-breathing **dragon**, like his **father**, into one of the kindest creatures that ever walked the planet. We kept being interrupted by animals from the forest who came over and thanked **Dragon Volcanic** for things he had done for them. It could have been **stage managed**, I suppose, but I very much doubt it. We had not publicised our meeting. It seemed **spontaneous** and of course we have **Mitor 113P's** personal **testimony** of **Dragon Volcanic's** caring personality. So I decided to allow the witness.

A tall thin wizard called **Wizard Polo Grub** stood up and said, in a high voice: 'Fine words, **Chief Wizard Grumptilian III**, but that's all they are. I think it is the height of irresponsibility, bringing this monster to our Hall. He could do anything and you would be powerless to stop him. How do you know that it is this **Dragon Volcanic**. I've never seen a **dragon** in the flesh before. It could be **Dragon Inferno** for all we know. How do you tell them apart? No, this trial is **untenable**. I move that we abandon it and get the hell out of here before we are fried to a crisp.'

CHIEF WIZARD GRUMPTILIAN III:
'Thank you, **Wizard Polo Grub**. You raise some valid points. I'll answer them in reverse order. When we were in the forest, **Dragon Volcanic** took us to see his mother, **Wendy**; a very nice **dragon**, just like her son, or should I say, he was just like her. I asked her about her husband, **Dragon Inferno** and she said we could have a look at him if we wanted. He wouldn't hurt us as he was asleep. She said he slept most of the time now. She left him food but he

hardly ever touched it. She didn't think he had long for this world. So she took us to his lair and, as she said, he was asleep. He is a bit bigger than **Dragon Volcanic** and his nostrils are red. As you can see, **Dragon Volcanic's** nostrils are blue. There is no doubt that the dragon standing before us was **Dragon Volcanic**.

As for your first point, **Wizard Polo Grub**, you are quite right. I cannot give any guarantees of **Dragon Volcanic's** good behaviour, but there comes a point where you have to make a decision and, on the **balance of probabilities**, I conclude that we are safe. However, this is a democracy and we will take a vote on it.

If you would like to continue with the trial, please raise your right hand.' 76 hands rose in the air.

CHIEF WIZARD GRUMPTILIAN III:
'Carried.'

WIZARD POLO GRUB: 'I don't care what you say, this trial is …

WIZARD 37: 'Shut up, **Polo**. We have to abide by the wishes of the majority. Either leave or sit down. You are making the place look untidy. Don't worry, we will look after you.'

Still grumbling, **Wizard Polo Grub** sat down.

OLD GRUMP: 'Are there any more objections? … No? … Carry on **Wizard Gyromuglan**.

WIZARD GYROMUGLAN: 'Will you tell us, **Dragon Volcanic**, when you first encountered **Wizard Zuron**?'

DRAGON VOLCANIC: 'I was playing in the forest when I saw this strange man and a donkey. I watched them for a while. They didn't look very fierce. I had never seen a man before, but I had seen plenty of monkeys. He looked similar, but not so hairy. I decided to frighten him away, like my **father** did. I leapt out onto the path in front of them, but I was too young to breathe fire, like my **father**; all I could manage was a puff of smoke. They laughed at me. I ran all the way home, crying, and told my **father** what had happened. He went mad and stormed off into the forest, looking for the man and his donkey. I went after him.'

WIZARD GYROMUGLAN: 'How old were you at the time?'

DRAGON VOLCANIC: '6 months.'

WIZARD GYROMUGLAN: 'Underline that, **Miss Jones**, would you? It's important.'

Miss Jones was the Clerk of the Council. She recorded the proceedings. 'Carry on, **Dragon Volcanic**.'

DRAGON VOLCANIC: '**Dad** caught up with the strange man in the clearing. He breathed fire on him and he shot up into the air and landed in the top of a tree. The man produced his own fire and brought a tree down on my **father**. It was a big tree. I think it must have winded him a bit, but he shook it off and breathed more fire on the man again. He leapt from tree to tree, then fell to the ground and didn't move. **Dad** picked him up and carried him to his lair. Whilst **Dad** was sleeping, me and **Mum** carried the man to **Mum's** cave. He's been there ever since. **Mum** found out from a troop of monkeys who had seen the whole thing, that the man was a **Wizard** called **Wizard Zuron**. I don't know how they knew that, but monkeys always seem to know everything.

WIZARD GYROMUGLAN: 'Did **Wizard Zuron** ever wake up?'

DRAGON VOLCANIC: 'No, he didn't. **Bonzo**, one of the monkeys, came and had a look at him and said he was dead. I take full responsibility for what happened; it should be me on trial today, not my **father.**'

CHIEF WIZARD GRUMPTILIAN III: 'Strike **Dragon Volcanic's** confession from the record, **Miss Jones**. It is not admissible. As a **minor** of 6 months he is not responsible for his actions before this court.'

DRAGON VOLCANIC: 'You mean I am in the clear?'

OLD GRUMP: 'Absolutely.'

Dragon Volcanic blew out a great plume of smoke from his nostrils. **The Wizards** sat back in their chairs, alarmed!

DRAGON VOLCANIC: 'Sorry about that, the smoke is harmless. It's just such a relief. I feel like a great weight has been lifted off my shoulders. Thank you, **Chief Wizard Grumptilian III**. Thank you very much indeed.'

OLD GRUMP: 'My pleasure, **Volcanic**. I would have said so before, but my hands were tied.'

He addressed the **Grand Council of Wizards**.

'So now we know, fellow **Wizards**, that **Wizard Zuron** did die from the fall, therefore **Dragon**

Inferno is not guilty of murder but he was **complicit** in his death, which makes him guilty of **manslaughter**. The maximum sentence for **manslaughter** is 15 years.'

DRAGON VOLCANIC: 'He won't last 15 weeks, let alone 15 years.'

OLD GRUMP: 'Quite! I anticipated this result and have been giving it a great deal of thought. Two days ago, I made a return visit to the forest specifically to talk to **Wendy**, **Dragon Volcanic's mother**. I asked about the health of her husband and she said he was deteriorating. I said to her: 'In view of his ill health, and the difficulties we would have in detaining him anywhere else, I was thinking of suggesting to the **Grand Council of Wizards** that we sentence **Dragon Inferno** to house arrest until he dies, but I need a jailer. **Wendy** thanked me for my **consideration**, which she said her husband did not deserve, but she could see why I suggested it. She said she would be his jailer; despite everything, she still loved him and would like to do this last thing for him.

So my recommendation to **The Grand Council** is to find **Dragon Inferno** guilty of **manslaughter** and sentence him to house arrest for the rest of his life. I throw it open for debate.'

WIZARD LUCIAN PLEBLUM: 'Far too **lenient.**'

WIZARD ARLIN FONTINBLADDER: 'Here, here. Far too **lenient.**'

WIZARD CRINGEWELL BILLYARSE: 'He's so ill, he won't even notice he's on house arrest.'
WIZARD MAGA LUFF: 'He needs to be punished.'

WIZARD GUNGADIN: 'Why don't we just kill him? It will be easier all round.'

CHIEF WIZARD GRUMPTILIAN III: '**Manslaughter** does not carry the death penalty.'

WIZARD GUNGADIN: 'No, but there are ways and means.'

WIZARD MAGA LUFF: 'You mean a hit man?'

WIZARD GUNGADIN: 'Why not?'

CHIEF WIZARD GRUMPTILIAN III: 'This is a court of law, **Wizard Gungadin**, not a **lynch mob**. Your road leads to **anarchy**; the Law of the Jungle – kill or be killed. Is that what you want?'

WIZARD GUNGADIN: 'No.'

WIZARD PONTIOUS MUGLAN: 'You are not on your own, **Wizard Gungadin**. Many of us feel the same way. If you remember, we debated this during the first trial, 40 years ago and we decided against it. I think we should vote on it again.'

CHIEF WIZARD GRUMPTILIAN III: 'It is most **irregular**, voting on something we cannot legally do, but I do remember **Wizard Pontious Muglan**, that my grandfather, **Chief** Wizard Grumptilian I did allow such a vote. So I suppose that sets a **precedent**. But I must stress that the vote is only **advisory**. It is not legally binding.

All those in favour of the death penalty being imposed on **Dragon Inferno**, raise your right hand.'

37 Wizards raised their hands.

CHIEF WIZARD GRUMPTILIAN III: 'Thank God for that! Motion defeated. Can we get back to the debate proper now?'

WIZARD FONTAINBLEU: 'We can't just leave him at home. He must go to jail.'

WIZARD IGNATIOUS CRIMPLE: 'Agreed. But what jail? Where would we put him?'

WIZARD FONTAINBLEU: 'There are dungeons in the basement of Fartigen University that we have used before.'

WIZARD IGNATIOUS CRIMPLE: 'True, but look at the size of **Dragon Volcanic**. **Dragon Inferno** is supposed to be even bigger. How would we get him in?'

WIZARD TONY PANDY: 'I can't think of any jail that would be big enough to take him. We would have to build something specifically to hold him.'

WIZARD PARAHANDY: 'If you did that, how would you get him there? How do you transport a 20 foot fire-breathing **dragon**?'

WIZARD FONTAINBLEU: 'We could put a bag on his head.'

WIZARD PARAHANDY: 'Some bag!'

WIZARD TONY PANDY: 'Why don't we build a jail in the forest where he lives?'

WIZARD PARAHANDY: 'From what **Chief Wizard Grumptilian III** has just said, **Dragon**

Inferno would probably be dead before we finish building the prison.'

WIZARD 37: 'Which brings us back where we started. I understand the **Grand Council's** reluctance to, as it sees it, allow **Dragon Inferno** to get away with killing **Wizard Zuron**. **Wizard Zuron** was a good friend of mine. I want justice for him as much as anybody else does. But we have to be practical. There isn't any realistic alternative to **Chief Wizard Grumptilian III's** proposed sentence of house arrest, which is why he is **Chief Wizard**. I suggest we vote on it.'

CHIEF WIZARD GRUMPTILIAN III: 'Thank you for that lukewarm endorsement of my mental powers, **Wizard 37**. Is everyone ready to vote?'

Murmurs of **assent**.

CHIEF WIZARD GRUMPTILIAN III: 'I'll take that as a Yes. All those who agree that **Dragon Inferno** is guilty of **manslaughter** and will be held in house arrest **indefinitely**, please raise your right hand.'

67 wizards raised their right hands.

OLD GRUMP: 'Carried. Good. I think that concludes the proceedings.'

WIZARD GYROMUGLAN: 'What about **Wizard Zuron?**'

OLD GRUMP: 'Oh yes, I do apologise. Would anyone like to see **Wizard Zuron?**'

WIZARD POLO GRUB: 'You mean he's here?'

OLD GRUMP: 'Oh yes.'

Wizard Gyromuglan walked over to a long table that was covered by a white sheet. He whipped off the sheet to reveal the skeleton of a man wearing a star spangled cloak of midnight blue.

OLD GRUMP: 'If you would like to pay your last respects to **Wizard Zuron**, gentlemen, please feel free to do so.'

The Wizards stood up, formed themselves into an orderly queue and slowly filed past the body of their dead colleague.

Scoby Breezly covered the trial for the Daily Scribbler. He had covered the first trial, 40 years ago. Or that's what he liked to say. He had actually been a **cub reporter** at the time. He had only been at the Daily Scribbler three weeks. **Dave Flett** was the chief reporter then. **Scoby** had persuaded him to let him be his 'bag man' and sit in on the trial. But it gave **Scoby the drop** on other reporters. No one else could remember the first trial. **Consequently**, his report was published by most newspapers on **Spug**. He became famous and was **feted** wherever he went.

Chapter Fifteen

Quite a party was travelling over the Silothan mountains. They were attending the Coronation of **Aloysius** and **Fancy** as **King** and **Queen of The Bonz**. In the party were **Professor Rumpant Pustule, QED** and **Tanganika**. **Rumpant** was considering retiring from Fartigen University and relocating to the Vushy Plain. Up until the arrival of **Tanganika**, **Rumpant** had been a confirmed bachelor and always thought he would remain one. His work was everything; it was his life. He was neither happy or sad, he was just content. But **Tanganika** had shown him that there were other things in life, more important than work. For the first time in his 60 odd years, he had fallen in love. **Tanganika** had become more important to him than his work. Apart from in his youth, he had never bothered much with girls, they didn't seem to understand him. But **Tanganika** seemed to know instinctively how to please him. It was the little things she did which fascinated him most as an **anthropologist**.

He loved the way she walked: she had an exaggerated hip movement which acted like a pivot for her legs, her feet moved across the ground smoothly. The action was very efficient, she didn't appear to be going fast, but **Rumpant** had a job to keep up with her when they were out. She looked like she could walk like that all day. It seemed effortless. She had a very expressive face, **Rumpant** could tell what she was thinking, just by looking at her face. Her obvious pleasure at seeing him, when he came home from work, brought a tear to his eye. He had never experienced that before.

Then there was her smile. She had a brilliant smile, not just one; she had half a dozen different smiles: from a broad grin to a little, thoughtful smile, that barely touched her lips, but was mostly in her eyes. But it was the way she looked after him that he loved the most. He had never had that before either.

Rumpant's mother had died when he was young. His father was always too busy to look after him, so he was passed between his aunts and uncles for most of his adolescent years. His aunts and uncles were very good to him, but there is no substitute for a mother's love. That's why he became an **anthropologist**, to try and make sense of it all: his father's **aloofness**, his aunt and uncles' **pity** and the fact that even though he could not remember his mother (he was two years old when she died), she was in his thoughts most days: whenever he bought something he thought: 'Would Mum have liked this?' He always wanted to please her. He always felt that he was missing something, but he didn't know what. Then **Tanganika** arrived and everything fell into place. He understood. It was love, of course; you had probably worked that out for yourself. It wasn't just the affection. **Tanganika** seemed to genuinely enjoy his company: she listened attentively when he talked about his work and asked intelligent questions. That was usually a big turn-off for his previous girlfriends, not that he had had many. They grew bored with him and dumped him. But not **Tanganika**. She found his **insights** into human behaviour fascinating and she had some **insights** of her own, that even surprised **Rumpant**, a **Professor** of 40 years' standing. She may not have had his qualifications, but **Rumpant** was clear that she was his equal. Plus she had an **intuition** which he did not possess, that often gave her an advantage over him.

Then there was the sex. But we won't go into that. It's not that kind of book.

Yet, despite all of that, **Rumpant** knew that **Tanganika** was not happy in Fartigen. She didn't like the big city, which is not surprising considering she had lived all her life in the depths of the Amazon Jungle. **Mrs Bridges** had befriended her and showed her how everything worked in the house. She was a quick learner. You only had to tell her once and she got it; you never had to tell her again.

On shopping trips, **Mrs Bridges** told **Rumpant** that **Tanganika** didn't like the crowds of people. She was **bamboozled** by all the shops and the thousands of things in them and she was frightened to death of the traffic. But **Tanganika** never once complained about it to **Rumpant**, not verbally anyway. But she couldn't help her **body language**. **Rumpant** was an expert in reading **body language**. It was an essential part of an **anthropologist's armoury**, and her **body language** was screaming at him: 'GET ME OUT OF HERE!'

Rumpant had the option of retiring at 60. He had never thought about retiring until **Tanganika** appeared on the scene. He had described to her **The Bonz**, **The Bonz Conundrums**, the Vushy Plain, **Wizard 37**, the Silothan Mountains, **Wizard**

Gyromuglan, and the **Mitor**s. She was very interested and asked lots of questions. She in turn, described her life in the Amazon Jungle, and her father who had met Wizard Zuron; she repeated her father's tales about Wizard Zuron.

Tanganika expressed a desire to see **The Bonz** for herself.

RUMPANT: 'I think you would like the Vushy Plain. There is plenty of space to roam about, very few people. **The Bonz** are no trouble, shy, but once they get to know you, you will have a friend for life. I have often thought that when I retire, I would like to relocate to the Vushy Plain, build a house next to **Wizard 37's** cottage.

TANGANIKA: 'I like the sound of that, **Rump**. I must admit, the city is not my favourite place.

RUMPANT: 'I know, you hate it, don't you?'

TANGANIKA: 'How do you know that? Has **Mrs Bridges** said something to you?'

RUMPANT: 'No, she didn't have to. It's written all over your face.'

TANGANIKA: 'It is quite uncanny how you know what I am thinking, **Rump**. I shall have to be careful. A girl needs to have a few secrets.'

They both laughed at that.

———————————

Dibert-Yon Longtooley, his wife **Yanilow** and their daughter **Oxana** were also in the party, as was **Shumpum Ballywater** and his wife, **Morwenna** and their son, **Sputnik**.

It had taken a good deal of persuading by **Dibert** to get **Yanilow** to come to the meeting with **Wizard Ariwold Grumptilian III**, Chancellor of Fartigen University. She didn't want to know at first, but he had worn her down. He had agreed a strategy with his mate **Shumpum Ballywater**: **Dibert** would say that **Shumpum's** wife, **Morwenna** was going, and **Shumpum** would say that **Yanilow** was going, even though neither of them knew anything about it. It's called playing one off against the other. By the time **Yanilow** and **Morwenna** discovered their husbands' little **ruse** it was too late. **Dibert** and **Shumpum** had accepted **Old Grump's** invitation, there was no going back on it. Then there was the problem of **Oxana** and **Sputnik**. Usually the two women babysat for each other, but as they were both going to the meeting, they would have to take the children with them. It was a good job they did. **Yanilow** and **Morwenna** were in a bad mood, having found out they had been **duped**, but they couldn't say anything in front of the children.

Old Grump showed them into his office. It was remarkably clean and tidy. His old desk had been cleared of its usual **detritus**, covered with a crisp white tablecloth, and was groaning with food. **Mrs Bridges'** doing, of course, aided and abetted by some of her girls. **Professor Rumpant Pustule** was there, together with the mysterious **Tanganika** who they had heard so much about. The rumours did not do her justice. She was even more beautiful in the flesh. She was a good 6 inches taller than **Rumpant**, and she was definitely not wearing high heels. They don't have high heels in the jungle.

There were two older gentlemen there as well, who **Dibert** and **Shumpum** didn't know, but had a pretty good idea who they were. They were **Wizard 37** and **Wizard Gyromuglan**. They were coming to Fartigen anyway for the trial of **Dragon Inferno**. **Old Grump** asked them to come a week early to help him prepare for the trial and meet **Dibert**, **Shumpum** and their families.

The food helped break the ice. It was delicious and the wine; there was pop for the children. After making the formal introductions, instead of making conversation with the adults, **Wizard 37** and **Wizard Gyromuglan** talked to the children. **Wizard 37** made them laugh, telling them all the funny things that **The Bonz** did. He showed them a picture of **The Bonz** and for his **piece de resistance**, produced two life-size cuddly toys of **The Bonz**. **Oxana** and **Sputnik** were overjoyed. **Wizard Gyromuglan** took over. He held the two children spellbound as he described flying over the Silothan Mountains suspended beneath two giant eagles called **Mitors**. They gazed at him, open-mouthed in **rapt wonderment**, their little faces were a picture of sheer joy. **Yanilow** and **Morwenna** melted. They couldn't do anything else. They had never seen the children so **captivated**. They were glad they came, but they were still going to give their husbands a **piece of their minds** when they got home.

The evening proceeded cheerfully after that. Everyone asked the two wizards questions about the

Vushy Plain, The Silothan Mountains, what it was like living there. **Rumpant** joined in, describing some of his studies of **The Bonz** and answering questions.

They had all had a really good evening, thoroughly enjoyed it. It had given them a great deal of **food for thought**. No decisions had been made yet, but they were headed in the right direction. It was gone midnight when they left. **Oxana** and **Sputnik** were fast asleep and had to be carried home by their dads.

———————

Rumpant was worried about taking such a large party over the Silothan Mountains. He was particularly concerned about the children. The weather in the mountains could turn in an instant. You often experienced all four seasons in one day. If a big storm blew up, he couldn't guarantee **Oxana** and **Sputnik's** safety. He passed an uncomfortable night. In the morning, **Tanganika** told him if he was that worried, he would have to tell **Dibert** and **Shumpum** that they couldn't bring the children, it was too dangerous. They both agreed that the children would be very disappointed but safety must come first. He was about to set off for their house when **QED** stopped him in the yard. **QED** had a very comfortable stable at the back of **Rumpant**'s house. **QED** ee-awed and told **Rumpant** that he needn't worry about the weather, the wizards had fixed it.

RUMPANT: 'What do you mean, the wizards have 'fixed it'? Wizards can't control the weather. They can cook up a storm, but that's about it. There is no way they could control the weather in the Silothan Mountains. It's too powerful, even for them.' **QED** couldn't explain how the wizards had done it; he didn't understand it himself. All he knew was that he had overheard **Wizard 37** and **Wizard Gyromuglan** saying that they were 'dead chuffed' that they would have good weather crossing the mountains.

Rumpant didn't know what to do. He wanted to believe **QED** but he didn't see how it was possible. Unfortunately, he couldn't contact the two wizards. They were busy preparing for the trial. After the trial **Rumpant** did manage to collar **Wizard Gyromuglan** outside **Tutuchamilabin** Hall. He told him of his concerns about taking such a large party over the Silothan Mountains and that he was particularly worried about the children. **Wizard**

Gyromuglan told him that it was alright – he and his fellow wizards had created a good weather corridor over the mountains. He could guarantee they would not have to endure any storms. **Rumpant** wanted to ask lots of questions, but **Wizard Gyromuglan** was too busy to explain. He said he had to go; they had a wizard to bury.

Wizard Gyromuglan was true to his word. As the party made its way over the Silothan Mountains, they were bathed in sunshine under a clear, blue sky. **Rumpant** had rarely experienced such good weather in the mountains, but this wasn't ordinary good weather, it was magic good weather. Either side of them billowed menacing dark storm clouds, but they were walking in a corridor of good weather. **Rumpant** asked **Wizard Gyromuglan** how he had done it.

WIZARD GYROMUGLAN: 'I couldn't do it on my own. After the trial of **Dragon Inferno**, the **Grand Council of Wizards** were so pleased to have finally brought him to justice, that I decided to chance my arm and asked them to do me a favour. I told them that a large party would be making its way over the Silothan Mountains for the Coronation of

Aloysius and **Fancy** as **King** and **Queen** of **The Bonz**. I asked them if they could combine their magic and create some sort of force field, that would allow safe passage over the mountains. You should never tell **The Council** what you want them to do – they don't like it. It is always best to let them decide (a) if they are willing to grant your request and (b) how they would do it.

They were only too pleased to grant my request and after much debate, decided to create two force fields, one either side of a ten foot corridor over the mountains. These force fields would extend above the cloud base and prevent any bad weather getting through. As you can see, that's exactly what we have got. We are bathed in sunshine whilst all around us storm clouds are brewing.'

RUMPANT: 'Remarkable. Quite remarkable. I didn't know such a thing was possible.'

WIZARD GYROMUGLAN: 'Neither did I, to be honest. But I had read about a similar thing that happened 2000 years ago when the Red Sea was parted.'

RUMPANT: 'How long will these force fields last?'

WIZARD GYROMUGLAN: 'Till we decide to get rid of them, I guess.'

RUMPANT: 'You mean they could last indefinitely?'

WIZARD GYROMUGLAN: 'I wouldn't say that, you know what magic is like. It could just go 'POP' and disappear. But there is over 100,000 years of experience in **The Grand Council of Wizards**. They have put together some powerful magic to create these force fields. It wouldn't surprise me if they lasted quite a while.'

RUMPANT: 'Great!'

THE BONZ

CORONATION

Chapter Sixteen

Fancy was nervous.

NOOLOO: 'Keep still, **Fancy**, or we are going to be here all day.'

FANCY: 'I can't keep still, **Nooloo**. I'm all of a **quiver**.'

Nooloo was trying to lace up **Fancy's** pink embroidered slippers. She was dressing her for her coronation. **The Bonz** don't generally go in for footwear for their little four toed feet, but the slippers were part of the **Queen's** robes. They were beautifully made. I'm not sure how old they were, but **Queen Bee** had worn them at her coronation; so had several queens before her. But they were tricky to fit with a lot of laces that had to be carefully threaded through the many eyelets.

FANCY: 'I wonder how **Ally's** getting on.'

NOOLOO: 'Don't worry about **Ally**. **Queen Bee** is looking after him. You don't mess with **Queen Bee**.'

A large crowd had gathered around the standing stone circle on the Vushy Plain. The **Mitors** were perched on top of the stones, keeping guard as they did for **the Bonz Conundrums**. The Coronation was to take place in the middle of the standing stones. Two elaborately carved thrones were positioned in the centre of the circle, with a table on each side. On top of the tables were two magnificent golden crowns beset with a multitude of coloured stones. The crown on the right was about twice the size of the one on the left.

Wizard 37 was stood to the right of the thrones in his full ceremonial **Wizard's** robes: deep red cloak, covered in silver stars and crescent moons and a matching pointed hat, with a large brim. In his hand he carried a golden **mace**. To the left was stood **Wizard Gyromuglan**, also in his full ceremonial **Wizard's** robes: sky blue cloak, covered in silver stars and wings and a matching pointed hat, with a large brim. In his hand he carried a golden **orb**.

The crowd parted and a magnificent gold and red open topped **landau** pulled by two magnificent little Falabella horses complete with their ostrich feather headdresses and magnificent gold and red covers on their backs, made its way, slowly, to the stone circle. The crowd clapped and cheered. **Aloysius** and **Fancy** were sat side by side in the **landau**, holding hands. With their other hands, they waved to the crowd. They had **butterflies** in their stomachs the size of **Mitors**. They were both very nervous, but elated at the same time. It didn't seem real, like something out of a dream. But it was real. It was very real indeed. In fact, the scene had hardly changed in the last thousand years.

Aloysius was wearing a magnificent gold and red cloak, trimmed in black and white **ermine**, and covered with **signs of the zodiac**. **Fancy's** cloak was similar, but covered in magnificent flowers, real ones.

The Falabella horses pulled **the landau** inside the stone circle and halted next to the thrones. **Wizard 37** helped **Aloysius** out and **Wizard Gyromuglan** helped **Fancy** out. They led them to their thrones: **Aloysius** to the one on the right and **Fancy** to the one on the left.

As soon as the **landau** entered the stone circle, a group of four **buglers** played a Fanfare to the Common Man. They continued to play until **Aloysius** and **Fancy** sat on their thrones. **Wizard 37** spoke to **Aloysius**: 'Do you, **Aloysius**,

Champion of the First Half of the First Quarter, **solemnly** swear to rule the Kingdom of the Vushy Plain **Bonz** with justice, fairness and **integrity**?'

ALOYSIUS: 'I do'

WIZARD 37: 'Do you, **Aloysius**, Champion of the First Half of the First Quarter solemnly swear to … I've forgotten what comes next.'

WIZARD GYROMUGLAN: (in a stage whisper) 'Keep the peace and come to the aid of your subjects in times of trouble'

ALOYSIUS: 'I do'

WIZARD 37: 'I think that will do.'

He picked up the crown, placed it on **Aloysius's** head and said: 'I, **Wizard 37**, crown you: **Aloysius, King of The Bonz**.'

The crowd clapped and cheered. **Wizard 37** handed **Aloysius** the golden **mace**. **Wizard Gyromuglan** spoke to **Fancy**: 'Do you, **Fancy**, Champion of the Second Half of the Third Quarter solemnly swear to aid your husband, **King Aloysius** in ruling the Kingdom of the Vushy Plain **Bonz** with justice, fairness, and **integrity**?'

FANCY: 'I do.'

WIZARD GYROMUGLAN: 'Do you, **Fancy**, Champion of the Second Half of the Third Quarter **solemnly** swear to aid your husband, **King Aloysius** to keep the peace and to come to the aid of your subjects in times of trouble?'

FANCY: 'I do.'

WIZARD GYROMUGLAN: 'There is supposed to be a bit about maintaining traditions, but **37** has forgotten that, so we'll pass on it.'

He picked up the crown, placed it on **Fancy's** head and said: 'I, **Wizard Gyromuglan**, crown you, **Fancy, Queen of The Bonz**.'

The crown clapped and cheered. **Wizard Gyromuglan** handed **Fancy** the golden **orb**. The crowd rushed inside the standing stone circle and surrounded the newly-crowned **King and Queen of The Bonz.**

Professor Rumpant Pustule, Tanganika, QED, Dibert-Yon Longtooley, Yanilow, Oxana, Shumpum Ballywater, Morwenna, Sputnik and **Chief Wizard Ariwold Grumptilian III** all watched in **wonderment** at the amazing brown furry animals. They thought: 'Surely there wasn't another sight on **Spug** to compare with this.'

Whilst he had them all together, **Wizard 37** took the opportunity of making an announcement to **The Bonz**.

WIZARD 37: 'My fellow **Bonz**. It is my sad duty to have to inform you that my time amongst you is drawing to a close. Soon, I will leave you for that Great Vushy Plain in the sky.'

Several **Bonz** cried out: 'No!' 'You can't!' 'What will happen?' 'We can't manage without you.'

But most simply burst into tears. Fighting back the tears himself, **Wizard 37** struggled on. 'I know, I know. I've been dreading this. But I must make provision for the future or everything will just **unravel**. You don't know him, but we are honoured to have with us today, the **Chief** of all the **Wizards** on **Spug**, none other than **Chief Wizard Ariwold Grumptilian III**.'

He indicated **Ariwold** with his hand. **Ariwold** performed an elaborate bow.

'**Chief Wizard Ariwold Grumptilian III** has selected a young **wizard** called **Wizard Dibert-Yon Longtooley**. I have been impressed by his intelligence and his attitude. In many ways, he reminds me of my younger self. He is a modest wizard. He doesn't seek **self-aggrandisement**, as many **wizards** do. He listens carefully and is ready to learn, but I will let you be the judge of his character. I have not made my decision yet on who will succeed me. I will listen to your views and, of course, the views of our new **King Aloysius** and **Queen Fancy**. **Dibert**, would you like to step forward and say a few words?'

Dibert stepped forward and stood beside **Wizard 37**.

DIBERT: 'I am not given to making grand speeches; as **Wizard 37** said, I am a modest man. I have read **Professor Rumpant Pustule's** bookon **The Bonz**, but meeting you in the flesh has been one of the highlights of my life. I think I can say the same for my wife, **Yanilow**, and my daughter, **Oxana**, hasn't stopped grinning since we got here. Obviously, I have a lot to learn; I wish the circumstances of my speaking to you today were not such a sad occasion. I have not known **Wizard 37** very long, but already he feels like a father figure to me. I see my duty as to serve, not to rule. If you chose to adopt me, I will work with **King Aloysius**

and **Queen Fancy** for the good of the Kingdom of the Vushy Plain **Bonz**.

Thank you. Please feel free to ask questions.

Wizard Gyromuglan and **Shumpum Ballywater** slipped away. They were heading for the mountains. In the **foothills** of the Silothan Mountains, **Wizard Gyromuglan** put two fingers in his mouth and gave a loud whistle. Two pairs of massive **Mitors** took off from one of the mountain peaks. They carried a long pole between them, clutched in their massive talons. Underneath the pole was slung a hammock. The Mitors didn't land, they hovered about three foot from the ground and allowed **Wizard Gyromuglan** and **Shumpum** to climb into the hammock. With a flap of their massive wings, the **Mitors** rose into the air.

As they approached the mountains, the **Mitors** circled round, gaining height on the **thermals**. When they were above the nearest peak, they spread their wings out and glided into the Silothan Mountain range.

Shumpum could have said something **momentous** about the exhilarating wonder of flying. He could have said something poetic about the stunning **majesty** of the snow- capped mountains. But he didn't ... he just went: 'Weeeeeeeeee! Altogether ... Weeeeeeeeeeee!'

THREE YEARS

LATER

Chapter Seventeen

Quite a community had built up around **Wizard 37's** old cottage. Another three cottages had been built. In the first one **Wizard Dibert-Yon Longtooley** and his wife **Yanilow** lived with their daughter **Oxana**, four and their son, **Baxted**, two. In the second cottage, **Wizard Shumpum Ballywater** and his wife **Morwenna** lived with their son, **Sputnik**, four and their daughter **Angeline**, two. In the third cottage **Professor Rumpant Pustule** and his wife **Tanganika** lived with their daughter, **Hula**, two.

Sadly, **Wizard 37** and **Wizard Gyromuglan** had both died. **Wizard Dibert-Yon Longtooley** had taken **Wizard 37's** place and **Wizard Shumpum Ballywater** had taken **Wizard Gyromuglan's** place. They had turned **Wizard 37's** old cottage into a school. With two **wizards**, two witches, a **professor** and **Tanganika,** they were not short of teachers.

Tanganika didn't have any qualifications like the others, but she taught the children invaluable skills like: how to live off the land, how to skin a rabbit, how to make and shoot a bow and arrow. Then there was her laugh: **Tanganika** could make you laugh just by giving you a funny look. They all loved **Tanganika**.

They called the school: Vushy Plain Primary School. They had seven pupils. If your maths is good, you are probably thinking: 'who are the extra two pupils?' They were **Frodo** and his sister **Meebee,** son and daughter of **King Aloysius** and **Queen Fancy**, **King** and **Queen** of **The Bonz**. Vushy Plain Primary School was the only school on **Spug** that had two brown furry animals in the class.

THE END

Master Cast List

in order of appearance

MITOR	Large eagle
THE BONZ	Large guinea pig
SPUG	The Magic Planet
DAD / KING ALOYSIUS	King of the Bonz
FRODO	King Aloysius's son
WIZARD 37	Wizard of the Bonz
WIZARD GYROMUGLAN	Wizard of the Silothan mountains
QUEEN FANCY	King Aloysius's wife
MEE BEE	King Aloysius's daughter
THE DUKE OF VUSHY	The Queen's husband when there is no king
KING CYRUS	The old King of The Bonz
QUEEN BEE	The Queen Mother
BIDDY	Female Champion Bonz Number 11
REEVE	Male Champion Bonz Number 12
QUALLOW	Female Champion Bonz Number 12
PIKE	Male Champion Bonz Number 21

LIVEY	Female Champion Bonz Number 21
PLUTO	Male Champion Bonz Number 22
VENUS	Female Champion Bonz Number 22
NUMPTY	Male Champion Bonz Number 31
INDY	Female Champion Bonz Number 31
TREV	Male Champion Bonz Number 32
FANCY	Female Champion Bonz Number 32
PLATO	Male Champion Bonz Number 41
PING	Female Champion Bonz Number 41
CRUST	Male Champion Bonz Number 42
NOOLOO	Female Champion Bonz Number 42
UMPIRE / PROFESSOR RUMPANT PUSTULE	Anthropologist from Fartigen University
NUMBER 22	Pluto's and Venus's family
THE HIGHLAND BONZ	Bonz that lived in the mountains

THE GRAND COUNCIL OF WIZARDS	All 100 Wizards of Spug
ARBUTHNOT	Hopeless ancient King of the Bonz
QED	Professor Rumpant Pustule's donkey
OLD FART	Nickname for Fartigen University
DR MARZIPAN	Rumpant's Tutor at Fartigen University
MASTER WIZARD ZURON	Wizard Explorer
DRAGON INFERNO	The biggest dragon of them all
DRAGON VOLCANIC	Dragon Inferno's son
GOVERNORS	Governors of Fartigen University
DIBERT-YON	Dibert-Yon Longtooley, Student wizard
SHUMPUM	Shumpum Ballywater, Student wizard
FOUNDING FATHERS	The original wizards who set up Fartigen University
YANILOW	Yanilow Longtooley, Dibert's wife
MORWENNA	Morwenna Ballywater, Shumpum's wife

THINGAMYBOB/OXANA	Dibert and Yanilow's daughter
SPUTNIK	Shumpum and Morwenna's son
DOCTOR	Fartigen G P
NED KELLY	Outlaw
THE TIN MAN	From the Wizard of Oz
WIZARD PANGALANG	Lecturer at Fartigen University
MRS BRIDGES / JOY	Cookery Teacher at Fartigen University
GRISELDA	Cookery student at Fartigen University
CLOIS	Cookery student at Fartigen University
BALLYWIN	Cookery student at Fartigen University
QUENLYN	Cookery student at Fartigen University
ROSILEA	Cookery student at Fartigen University
REG DWIGHT	Elton John
NORMA JEAN	Marilyn Monroe
OLD GRUMP / ARIWOLD	Chief Wizard Ariwold Grumptilian III, Head of the Council of Wizards and Chancellor of Fartigen University

WIZARD FONTAINBLEU	Wizard of the Pyrenees mountains
BORIS	Wizard Borodin's dog
MICHELLE	Wizard Fontainbleu's girlfriend
WIZARD MAGNANAMUS	Old Chancellor of Fartigen University
MARCEL	Wizard Fontainbleu's assistant
PLANET ZOG	The most terrible place you could NOT imagine
THE UMPIRE	Independent Fartigen University wizard
PRINCESS SAMANTHA	Wizard Boradin's daughter
JEEVES	Wizard Boradin's butler
CORDWANGLE	Wizard Boradin's lute player
SCOBY BREEZLY	Journalist for The Daily Scribbler
TUTUCHAMILABIN	Spug's proper name
TANGANIKA	6 foot 4 inch Amazonian beauty
HIPPOLYTE	Tanganika's husband
BREMUSA	Witch Doctor
ORITHA	Tanganika's father
AELLO	Warrior

PENTHESILEA	Warrior
KLEOPTOLENE	Tanganika's friend
CLETE	The Chief
FATHER MCKENZIE	Cistercian monk in charge of the Amazon Mission
DR ROBERTSON	Doctor from Fartigen University on temporary secondment to the Mission
AINIA	Village old woman
DEINOMACHE	Village old woman
THE WIZARDS	All 100 wizards of Spug
WENDY / MUM	Dragon Volcanic's mother, Dragon Inferno's wife
MITOR 113P	Large eagle
MISS JONES	Clerk of the Council of Wizards
WIZARD POLO GRUB / POLO	Wizard of Grub
BONZO	Monkey
WIZARD LUCIAN PLEBLUM/W1	Wizard of things that go bump in the night
WIZARD ARLIN FONTINBLADDER / W2	Wizard of Lost causes
WIZARD CRINGEWELL BILLYARSE / W3	Wizard of bad smells
WIZARD GUNGADIN	Wizard of Lost Causes

WIZARD PONTIOUS MUGLAN / W9	Wizard of Dreams
WIZARD IGNATIOUS CRIMPLE / W6	Wizard of Montelemar
WIZARD TONY PANDY / W7	Wizard of the Great Orme
WIZARD PARAHANDY / W8	The practical wizard
DAVE FLETT	Old Chief Reporter for the Daily Scribbler
BAXTED	Dibert and Yanilow's son
ANGELINE	Shumpum and Morwenna's daughter
HULA	Rumpant and Tanganika's daughter

Master Words List

in order of appearance

thermals	upward current of warm air used by birds to gain height
talons	sharp claws
distraction	an agitated mental state
homing	return of an animal, by instinct, to its territory
sheepish	showing embarrassment from shame or shyness
wits' end	completely at a loss as to what to do
modicum	a small quantity
The Bonz Conundrums	set of confusing and difficult problems and questions
umpire	an official who watches a game or match closely to enforce the rules
zip wire	cable stretched between two points of different heights down which a person slides for amusement by means of a suspended harness, pulley or handle
nowt	nothing
crabby	bad tempered, irritable

incest	sexual relations between people classed as too closely related to marry each other
essence	critically important
anthropology	the study of human behaviour
delusions of grandeur	unrealistic social importance
consequently	as a result
wallop	strike or hit very hard
conflab	an informal private conversation or discussion
hair trigger	trigger of a firearm set for release at the slightest pressure
gingerly	in a careful or cautious manner
sight	a device on the crossbow used for assisting in precise aim
glowered	have an angry or sullen look on one's face
honorary	title given to someone held in great respect
sought	looked for
deceptively	to a greater extent than appears the case
conferring	have discussions
elect	elected to a position but not yet in office
aloft	overhead

gene pool	the different genes in an interbreeding population
nocturnal	active at night
not the sharpest knife in the drawer	not very bright
sanction	official permission or approval of an action
reconvene	bring together for a meeting
palaver	prolonged and tedious fuss or discussion
rogue	animal with destructive tendencies
willy nilly	whether one likes it or not
indubitably	absolutely
cumbersome	slow, complicated and therefore inefficient
unerring	they always succeed
knack	tendency to do something
chin wag	talk
VIB	Very Important Bonz
surplus to requirements	not needed any more
gooseberry	third person in the company of two others, especially lovers who would prefer to be alone
sewn on	guaranteed
besotted	strongly infatuated

wistfully	having a feeling of vague or regretful longing
morse code	a code in which letters are represented by a combination of long and short sounds
pull the wool over	deceive someone
cushy number	easy job
characteristic	a feature or quality belonging typically to a person to identify them
broached	raise a sensitive subject for discussion
crestfallen	sad and disappointed
social engineering	the use of centralised planning in an attempt to manage social change and regulate the future development and behaviour of a society
ventured	undertake a risky or daring journey or courseof action
ferocious blizzards	violent snow storm
searing	burn or scorch with intense heat
superstition	widely held but irrational belief in supernatural influences
fantasy	the faculty or activity of imagining improbable things
throw down the gauntlet	issue a challenge

infidel	a person who has no religion
shimmering	shine with a soft tremulous light
iridescent	showing luminous colours that seem to change when seen from different angles
adversary	opponent
zinging	quality or characteristic that excites interest
motionless	not moving
jungle telegraph	passed on by word of mouth
begged to differ	disagreed
thorn in their side	source of continual annoyance or trouble
constitution	a body of fundamental principles or established precedents according to which a state or organization is governed
gastronomy	the practice or art of choosing, cooking and eating good food
chip off the old block	someone who resembles their parents character
crowned	hit on the head
noddle	a person's head
resin	sticky substance used by weightlifters to get a good grip
turban	man's headdress

put our thinking caps on	meditate on a problem
parlous	full of uncertainty, precarious
domestic machinations	family plot or schemes
province	an area within which one has special knowledge
needs must	it is necessary or unavoidable
wuss	a weak or ineffectual person
becomes you	does you credit
accolade	something granted as a special honour in
	recognition of merit
abracadabra	word said by conjurors when performing a magic trick
bickering	argue about petty or trivial matter
precedent	an earlier event or action serving as an example or guide
magnitude	importance
paucity	the presence of something in only small or insufficient amounts
whim	sudden desire or change of mind, especially one that is unusual or unexplained
fancy	superficial or transient feeling of attraction

deed poll	a legal deed executed by one party only, to formalise a change in a person's name
Bob's your uncle	used to express ease with which a task can be acheived
double barrelled	name having two parts joined by a hyphen
low ebb	in a poor state
post-natal depression	depression after giving birth
hide your light under a bushel	keep your abilities or good qualities hidden from other people
pigs might fly	no chance
maudlin	self pityingly or tearfully sentimental
immortal	living forever
reprobates	an unprincipled person
mortality	the state of being subject to death
auspices	with the support or protection of
kilter	out of harmony or balance
mundane	lacking interest or excitement
soporific	inducing drowsiness or sleep
delectations	pleasure and delight
presumptuous	failure to observe the limits of what is
	permitted or appropriate

Hippocratic oath	an oath affirming the cook's obligations and proper conduct
Pray, proceed	Please carry on
whipper snappers	inexperienced, keen young wizards
hoola hoop	large plastic ring
inconsolable	not able to be comforted
wild goose chase	pointless search
fortuitous	happening by a lucky chance
a little bird tells me	I heard a rumour
soiree	evening party or gathering, typically in a Private house
tardiness	delayed beyond the right time, late
chivalric	the medieval knightly system with itsreligious, moral and social code of honour
conceive	become pregnant
quirk of fate	a strange chance occurrence
rampaged	rushed around in a violent and uncontrollable manner
semaphore	a system of sending messages by holding of the arms of two flags in certain positions in accordance to an alphabetic code
ebbed	gradually decreased
wreak havoc	widespread destruction

adamant	refusing to be persuaded to change one's mind
anti-social behaviour	contrary to the customs of society and causing annoyance and disapproval in others
soft target	easy to attack
edifice	large imposing building
enslaving	making someone a slave
will	control or constraint deliberately exerted
outraged	extremely strong reaction of anger or indignation
prevaricating	speaking or acting evasively
pergola	arched structure forming a framework for climbing plants
cronies	close friends or companions
debacle	utter failure or disaster
generous to a fault	freely giving more of something than is necessary or expected
confronted	stand/ meet face to face with hostile intent
duel	prearranged contest with deadly weapons between 2 people to settle point of honour
nip this in the bud	suppress or destroy something early on
consult	seek information or advice from

duffers	incompetent or stupid people
discomknockerating	enormously astounding
rumply	sexy
witty	showing or characterised by quick and inventive humour
renegade	a person who deserts a set of principles
scruples	feeling of doubt or hesitation with regard to the morality or propriety of an action
shenanigans	mischief
compelling	bringing about by force or pressure
riddles	a question or statement phrased so as to require ingenuity in ascertaining its answer or meaning
pettifogging	petty or trivial
aggrandizements	artificial enhancements of Maga Luff's reputation
mischievous	playful misbehaviour
extracurricular activities	something outside your course or career
crux	decisive or most important point at issue
motivated	a reason for doing something
sterling	excellent, of great value
suffused	gradually spread through or over

nemesis	inescapable agent of someone's downfall
doused	extinguished fire with water
imperceptibly	slight, gradual
entranced	filled with wonder and delight
adversary	opponent
crowned	the top part of a person's head
trident	three pronged spear
genesis	the origin or mode of formation of something
simultaneously	done at the same time
transfixed	motionless with wonder and astonishment
apparition	remarkable thing making a sudden appearance
ecky thump	blooming heck
de-activate	make something inactive or destroy it
afflictions	cause of pain or harm
obliged	legally or morally bound to do something
portcullis	a strong, heavy grating that can be lowered down in grooves on each side of a gateway to block it
abode	house or home

put people's backs up	annoy them
appease	placate somebody by acceding to their demands
sycophantic	a toady, a servile flatterer
appeasements	a number of attempts to appease
scorn	statement or gesture showing contempt
histrionics	exaggerated or dramatic behaviour
avidly	keenly interested or enthusiastic
lute	stringed instrument with a long neck, a rounded body and a flat front, played by plucking
ridiculing	mockery or derision
prowess	bravery in battle
bit your hand off	accepted with alacrity, brisk and cheerful readiness
by the cringe	an expression of amazement
obnoxious	extremely unpleasant
mojo	confidence
pendulum	weight hung by a fixed point so that it can swing freely
his eyes glazed over	he was bored, thinking of something else
dilemma	situation in which a difficult choice has to be made between two alternatives

entitled	has a right
title	word used before a person's name indicating their official rank
impossible	very difficult to deal with
vigorously	in a way that involves physical strength, effort or energy, strenuously
dark horse	person about whom little is known but who unexpectedly succeeds
spasms	sudden involuntary muscular contractions or convulsive movement
infectious	likely to spread or influence others
implored	beg earnestly or desperately
mauled	wounded by scratching and tearing
countenance	admit as acceptable or possible
mixed metaphor	a figure of speech in which a word or phrase is applied to something to which it is not literally applicable
duration	time during which something continues
niceties	the customary code of polite behaviour in society
elapsed	passed
rubbed along	cope or get along with, without undue difficulty

untenable	unable to be maintained or defended against attack or objection
vengeance	punishment inflicted or retribution exacted for an injury or wrong
swamp	an area of waterlogged ground
prevailed	persisted to do something
litter	framework with a couch for transporting the sick
canny	having and showing shrewdness and good judgement
collapsed	suddenly fell down
chastity	the state or practice of abstaining from sexual relations
calling card	business card
copper plate	a style of neat, round, handwriting, usually slanted and looped
astray	become lost or mislaid
buzzard	large hawk-like bird of prey with broad wings and a rounded tail
job lot	group of articles bought at one time
dissuade	persuade someone not to take a course of action
avuncular	like an uncle in being kind and friendly towards a younger or less experienced person

resplendent	attractive and impressive through being colourful or sumptuous
well founded	based on good evidence or reasons
regarding	gaze at in a concerned way
malevolent	wishing evil to others
habitual	done constantly or as a habit
spirits	the non-physical part of a person which is the seat of emotions and character regarded as surviving after death of body
diplomatically	tactfully
exploits	bold and daring feats
consequently	as a result
honour	under a moral obligation to carry out
torrential	an overwhelming outpouring
platonic	intimate and affectionate love but not sexual
contend	struggle to surmount
distraught	extreme anxiety, sorrow, pain
lair	a wild animal's resting place
nap	short sleep especially during the day
rampaged	rush around in a violent and uncontrollable manner
off-limits	out of bounds

transgressed	go beyond the limits set by principle
on the other hand	all things considered
inflict	cause something unpleasant to be suffered by someone else
sceptical	inclined to question or doubt
fledged	ready to fly
ballistic	fly into a rage
tirade	long speech of angry criticism or accusation
living daylights	to beat someone with great severity
ravenously	voraciously hungry
infidel	a person who has no religion
goner	dead
regalia	distinctive clothing and trappings of high office worn at formal occasions
apparent	readily perceived or understood
transfixed	rooted to the spot
shimmering	shine with a soft tremulous light
iridescent	showing luminous colours that seem to change when seen from different angles
stage managed	arranged carefully to create a certain effect
testimony	formal statement

untenable	not able to be maintained or defended against attack or objection
spontaneous	open, natural, and uninhibited
balance of probabilities	in a civil trial, one party's case need only be more probable than the other
minor	person under the age of legal responsibility
complicit	involved in an unlawful activity
manslaughter	the crime of killing a human being without malice aforethought
consideration	thoughtfulness towards others
lenient	merciful
lynch mob	band of people intent on killing someone for an alleged offence
anarchy	state of disorder due to absence or non-recognition of government or other controlling system
irregular	contrary to a rule
precedent	an earlier event or action that is regarded as an example or guide to be considered in subsequent similar circumstances
advisory	having power to make recommendations but not to take action enforcing them

assent	expression of approval or agreement
indefinitely	lasting for an unknown or unstated time
cub reporter	junior reporter
the drop	advantage over
consequently	result or effect
feted	everyone wanted to talk to him
aloofness	distant
pity	feeling of sorrow or compassion caused by the sufferings of others
insights	capacity to gain an accurate and deep
intuition	understanding of something, ability to understand something immediately, without the need for conscious reasoning
bamboozled	mystified
body language	the conscious and unconscious body movements and posture by which feelings are communicated
armoury	an array of resources available for a particular purpose
ruse	stratagem or trick
duped	deceive or trick
detritus	debris

piece de resistance	the most important or remarkable feature of a creative work
rapt wonderment	fully absorbed and intent, fascinated, awed admiration
captivated	attract and hold the interest and attention of, charm
piece of their mind	tell them what they thought, forcefully
food for thought	something that warrants serious consideration
quiver	shake or tremble with a slight rapid motion
mace	staff of office, heavy club with a metal head
orb	golden globe surmounted by a cross, forming part of the regalia of a monarch
landau	horse drawn, four wheeled enclosed carriage
butterflies	fluttering and nauseous sensation felt in the stomach when one is nervous
ermine	the white winter fur of the stoat used for trimming ceremonial robes
signs of the zodiac	star signs
buglers	play a brass instrument like a small trumpet, traditionally used for military signals

solemnly	deeply sincere
integrity	having strong moral principles
wonderment	state of awed admiration and respect
unravel	begin to fail or collapse
self-aggrandisement	artificial enhancement of one's reputation
foothills	low hills at the base of a mountain range
momentous	of great importance or significance
majesty	impressive beauty

Available worldwide from Amazon
and all good bookstores

—————————

Michael Terence
Publishing

www.mtp.agency

mtp.agency

@mtp_agency